Martini Girl
and other stories

A collection of seven quick reads

from the author

of

'The House Fell on Her Head'

Praise for *The House Fell on Her Head*:

'A gripping and enthralling take on World War Two.'

(Nick Louth, bestselling author of *Bite, Heartbreaker,* and *Mirror Mirror*)

'Fascinating details of World War Two so vividly described.'

(Bryony Doran, author of *The China Bird*)

'Intriguing characters and psychology. Ranges skilfully over time and place.'

(Jane McLaughlin, author of *Lockdown, The Abbott's Cat*)

'An accomplished and page turning debut novel.'

(Susan Elliott Wright, bestselling author of *What She Lost, The Things We Never Said, The Secrets We Left Behind*)

'...meticulously researched... deftly told... dialogue that crackles with tension and humour'

(Marian Dillon, author of *Looking for Alex, The Lies Between Us*)

'A fascinating mystery.'

(Michelle Pashley, author of *Black Sheep Cottage*)

'Gripping, atmospheric, original, vivid.'

(Karola Gajda, author of *Are My Roots Showing*)

'What a page turner. A very original story.'

(Lizzy Lloyd, author of *The Whyte Hinde*)

Credits:

Joyriding was first published by *Mslexia,* Issue 73 (2017)

An earlier version of *The Last Post* was published in the *Lincolnshire Echo,* 2011

Sand, and *Second Honeymoon,* were first published by www.cutalongstory.com, 2017

Acknowledgements:

With thanks to Jane McLaughlin, for her perspicacity and tireless attention to both structure and content in editing these stories; and writer friends for their forbearance and feedback as I experimented with the ideas and characters and earlier versions of what became the stories in this collection.

Contents

Martini Girl

He puts the folder on the table and checks his notebook. 'The practice nurse reported bruising to your father's arms and legs.'

She steps backwards. The edge of the chair meets the back her knees, and she sits, hands on her lap, picking her nails. He remains standing. She feels stupid now, for being so welcoming. She thought maybe they were here to help, invited them in, asked if they wanted a cup of tea. He pretended he did, but it was a trick to get her in the kitchen, while his colleague went into the living room. She can hear them, talking. It makes sense now, the look on the practice nurse's face yesterday, as she asked her to wait outside, and again, when she brought her father through to the waiting room. He was smiling, waving at the receptionist as they left. 'Goodbye, Mr Tunnicliffe. Look after yourself, now,' turning to her colleague, smiling, Elspeth could imagine her saying, 'He's such a charmer, that Mr Tunnicliffe'.

'Elspeth. Can I call you Elspeth?'

No, you can't, it's Miss Tunnicliffe; but even though he's at least twenty years her junior, she recognises his authority, standing there with his notebook and pen, and she's – what is she? He knows nothing about her, she's just her father's carer.

'Have you any idea how this could have happened, Elspeth?'

She'd wondered that, herself, when she saw the row of little bruises on his upper arm, blue in the centre with concentric outer circles in shades of purple. How could that have happened? 'Perhaps he fell? Yes, he trips sometimes, his feet don't move quite as fast as they used to.' She can hear those feet, coming up the stairs, across the landing, getting closer…

The young man holds his head on one side, listening. Not judging. He nods and writes a few words. 'Can you remember, Elspeth, if your father fell recently?'

It was a few days ago, when she was helping him to get out of the bath. There was a puddle of water on the floor, and he slipped. She says this.

—

He's frowning, his head still on one side. Such a nice young man. If he has a girlfriend, or a wife, at home, she wonders if she knows how lucky she is. 'I'm trying to understand, you see, Elspeth, how those particular bruises could be the result of a trip or a fall. Because most of the bruises are on his upper arms. They're like' – putting his pen between his teeth, he wraps his right hand around the fleshy upper of his left arm, then takes his pen back, makes a note – 'fingertip bruising, as though he's been gripped, really hard?'

It's a question, inviting her to think about whether she gripped him, and maybe she did, she can't remember, but she can imagine grasping at the slippery, fleshy body as it slid through her hands. 'I must have got hold of him, to pull him up when he tripped. He's a heavy man, though not as big as he was, not very steady on his feet.' *The whole house shakes with those feet, stamping up the stairs, and I shake, listening to them, waiting, sitting on the floor by the bed. What have I done? I can't think straight, because my head is full of the sound of feet, coming closer....*

He nods. 'I see that. Yes. Pulling him up could do that. And do you think he might have got the bruises on his legs when he fell? Did he fall against

—

9

something?' He believes her, he's helping her out, now.

'He was wedged, between the bath and the toilet. Maybe…?' It's coming back now. But, surely, she pulled him up by the hands, not by the arms?

He turns his head towards the sound of laughter from the living room, then smiles at her. 'He's on good form, your father.' He makes a few more notes, closes the file. 'I'll record our conversation, and I'll speak to my colleague.' He points at the blister on the back of her hand. 'That looks nasty.' She pulls her cuff down, to cover it. With the file now in his bag he goes into the hallway, looks around the living room door. She hears his colleague, laughing, 'I'll remember that, Mr Tunnicliffe. It's been lovely to meet you'.

Back on the doorstep, he looks up at her from the same position as twelve minutes ago; that's all it took. 'Thank you, Elspeth, for your time. Most likely it'll be fine, the account you've given, we just have to check with a manager.' Behind her, his colleague comes out of the living room. 'You'll understand that we need to follow these things up. It's hard, looking after older people, they can be challenging, we need to know if more support can be put in place, to help you.'

He doesn't wait to hear whether she does want more support. She's still shaking her head, saying, 'No thanks, Dad won't have strangers in the house,' as the two of them walk down the path, opening their diaries; she is forgotten. She closes the door, peers into the living room. He's scrolling through the TV guide.

'All right, Dad?'

'What was all that about?'

'Your bruises, Dad, on your arms and legs, there seem to be more, how did that happen?'

'Nosey bastards. She wanted to know if anyone had hurt me. I didn't say anything. Don't want them sneaking around in my business. But you'd better watch it, young lady.' He smirks at her then looks back at the television.

Young lady. From the doorway, she can see her reflection in the mirror above the mantelpiece. Two missed salon appointments and her hair is lank, with a margin of grey roots down the middle. Small eyes are made even smaller by blue pouches like bruises encircling her eyes, and there are new lines around her mouth. Leaning her head on the doorpost, she closes her eyes. She could sleep, right here…

'Don't just stand there. It's half past ten and I haven't seen any coffee yet.'

'I'll get the kettle on.' As she walks into the kitchen, the volume is turned up behind her and studio laughter fills the hallway between them. It's the boxed set of DVD s – TV games and quizzes – that she bought him for Christmas. She knows them all, off by heart. This one is Family Fortunes. She takes in the tray, with coffee, and the shopping list.

'Look at that, I got all of them,' he chuckles, pointing his cigarette at the television. When she doesn't respond, he says, 'Names of football clubs – they didn't get Villa, or Athletic. But I did. I got them all. See, you,' he jabs his cigarette at her and she steps back. 'You think you're so clever with your fancy job, but you wouldn't have got them, would you?'

'No Dad, I wouldn't. Anything particular you fancy for supper?' She raises her voice to compete with the television.

'Pasty and chips. With mushy peas.'

She writes on her list. 'I'm off to the shops.'

He pulls himself up, reaches for his walking stick. 'I'm coming with you.'

That sinking feeling as her hour of freedom slips away. 'It's very cold outside. I think it's going to rain.'

'I need some cash. It's pension day.'

'I can go to the post office for you.'

'Help yourself, more like.'

'Why would I do that, Dad? I've got my own money. I don't want yours.'

'Well, it's going somewhere.'

Elspeth knows the pools man came yesterday and took the money for a month of entries, and said he'd put a bet on for him; she saw him hand over a twenty-pound note.

Pushing the wheelchair down the hill to the shops, she remembers a game her mother used to play: letting her pushchair go, on this slope, so it went fast, and faster, and she'd scream with excitement and terror, then suddenly, her mother was there, in front of her, smiling, stopping the pushchair, leaning over her, rubbing noses, laughing. Her mother's face. Always, with the face comes the memory of his voice screaming, 'Get out, get out, you fucking jezebel.' She thinks of letting go of the wheelchair, watching it hurtle down the hill, faster, flying off the kerb and under the bridge, across the main road…

'Not so bloody fast.' He's sitting forward, his woollen gloves on the wheels to slow them down. She smiles to herself at the hint of panic in his voice. But slows the pace.

Outside the post office, she parks him by the steps and reaches to take his pension book from him, but he pulls it away and presses the button by the door, 'For Assistance' and in a few seconds a clerk comes out.

'Hello, love, how's that young man of yours, treating you right?' He winks and the clerk colours and giggles. He holds out his book.

'You're looking well, Mr Tunnicliffe, but maybe you shouldn't be out in this cold weather.'

'Got to keep an eye on her, in case she makes off with my pension.'

The young woman glances at Elspeth, as though she might believe him, and goes back inside. Within a few minutes she's back, counting money into his palm. He makes a show of counting it again, and pushes it into his inside pocket.

He winks at the clerk. 'Remember what I said, if

he doesn't give you satisfaction, you know my address.'

Elspeth mouths, 'sorry,' over his head but the young woman doesn't look at her.

'Bye, bye, Mr Tunnicliffe,' she smiles and waves and turns back into the post office.

Further along, he wants to go into the butcher's. 'I'll get some proper bacon, not that streaky muck you buy.'

The butcher stops serving to come round the counter, to the door, to lift the front of the wheelchair over the step. 'Good to see you out and about, Mr Tunnicliffe. How are you?'

'Mustn't grumble.'

'Maybe you should get one of those mobility scooters.'

'Might be a bit safer than her driving.' He indicates Elspeth with his thumb, and they laugh.

'Good to see you've not lost your sense of humour,' says the butcher.

In the Spar, her father flirts with the middle-aged woman behind the counter. Elspeth thinks she recognises her, says 'Hello' and is ignored. She feels she has become the invisible pusher of the wheelchair, the carrier of bags which cut red welts into her wrists as they fill with magazines, sausages, cornflakes, tins of soup.

The uphill slope back to the house is tough going. Although it's cold, and drizzling, and she can only see a few yards through the fog, she is sweating and stops to open her coat.

'Don't hang them bags on the handles, they bang against the wheels.'

The phone is ringing as she opens the front door. Leaving him in the wheelchair she rushes to answer it.

'It's a quick courtesy call, Elspeth' – she recognises the young social worker's voice – 'To say I'm going to drop in some information and an application form, for the day centre, that might be of interest to you?'

'Oh, yes, please.' She closes her eyes, thinking, a whole day without… A sudden, sharp pain in her foot makes her take a deep breath and she feels him standing beside her. He is leaning on his stick. Through the pain, she says, 'Thank you, that would–' before he knocks the phone from her ear with his free hand. As the social worker says goodbye, she realises the phone is still switched to loudspeaker, the way he likes it.

'Don't think you're going to palm me off with a pile of geriatrics.' He lifts the stick off her foot and turns and limps into the living room. 'And turn the bloody heating up, it's fucking arctic in here thanks to you leaving the door open.' He slams the living room door and within seconds she hears the 'Blankety Blank' jingle at maximum volume.

Elspeth hauls the wheelchair into the hallway and the bags into the kitchen and unpacks as she daydreams a phone call from her other world. 'Hello, Elspeth, we are missing you, when are you coming back to work?' No, that suggests a certain informality, the kind of relationship that Elspeth keeps at bay, at work. It's more likely to be, 'Miss Tunnicliffe, can I review your appointments diary for tomorrow to fit in an urgent meeting with the architect about the new City property?' That would feel real, important, as though she mattered, help her to remember who she is and where she belongs. She sits at the table, resting her forehead in her hands, listening to the blood pumping and whooshing through her head. She could sleep, like this, like — *Girl, where's my dinner, you've been down that café again, playing fast and loose I shouldn't wonder. Like mother, like daughter. Martini Girl, anytime, anyplace—*

Bang, bang, bang. 'Girl, I said, when's dinner around this fucking gaff?' He's standing over her, his walking stick laid across the table in front of her, banging it down.

Girl? She thinks, I'm forty-seven, nearly fifty years old and look at me.

'Fat lot of use you are, fast asleep when you're supposed to be looking after me and it's more like me, looking after you. No wonder you can't find a man.'

I can't find a man because — because— She's up and opening a tin of soup. 'Go and sit down, Dad, I'll bring it through.'

Over his shoulder, he says, 'And don't think this house is ever going to be yours. I'm leaving it to the bloody dogs' home.'

Leaning against the sugar bowl is the social worker's card. She fingers it. Perhaps a phone call, to say she can't cope, send help.

'I have to get back to work,' is what she says, when she takes the tray in and places it on his lap. 'I can't stay after the weekend.'

'Don't give me that. I know for a fact that your boss is allowing you another two months off. Carer's leave, isn't that what he calls it? He says they can manage. He's probably glad to see the back of you, useless that you are–'

'When did you speak to my manager?'

'Can't think.' He takes his time, pulling off a hunk of bread, dipping it in the tomato soup, sucking it noisily, licking his lips. 'Might have been yesterday that he rang. You must have been out, going for your 'bit of fresh air' in the park.' He sneers. 'Tch, I know about your fresh air–'

'I'll ring him back.'

'Don't bother. We had a good talk, him and me. Posh, isn't he, this boss of yours? "Call me Jim", he says, and "Don't worry, Mr Tunnicliffe, I can see your need is greater than ours. You tell Elspeth that I'll authorise maximum carer's leave."' He pushes another hunk of bread into his soup, stirs it around, scoops a pile of orange mush onto his spoon and slurps it. The liquid drips from his lips, onto his jumper.

'You didn't tell me.'

'I thought I'd see how long you kept up this performance.' He puts on a falsetto, whingeing voice. '"Got to get back for my job," and, "I have important contracts in the City. They'll be missing me. I'm a highfalutin, fancy bint that puts it out for–" Don't walk away from me, Girl.'

She wonders when he last used her given name. *Girl, you, tramp, ugly…*

Upstairs, in the back bedroom, she can hear him chuckling, below. There is nothing of her, left here. What she didn't take, in her suitcase at seventeen, he threw away or burned. She sits on the airbed that she bought after the first uncomfortable night on the settee. Why did she come back? The dutiful Christmas and birthday visits, never staying more than an hour or so – that's how long it took him to start the old pattern of demand and insult – had lasted for almost thirty years. Until that phone call, to say he'd had a stroke, could go home if he had someone there. Could she have said no?

Her foot is bruised and painful. She looks up the symptoms on her phone. It feels as though it's damaged one of her tendons. She examines the blister on her hand and rubs the other 'accidental' cigarette burn on her elbow. Tears sting the backs of her eyes, tears of tiredness and pain and frustration. Nothing has changed. Except now she has a life to lose, a life far away from here, where she is liked, respected. That is, until he spoke to her manager. What else did he say? Should she phone the office? She picks up her phone, reads the emails from her friends in the Soroptimist Club, keeping her in the loop, arranging theatre tickets, shopping trips, and some of them have sent texts, glad to hear she's enjoying some quality time with her poor old dad.

'Where do you think you're going?' he shouts from the living room as she opens the front door. 'Come and get this tray.'

The practice nurse is on the doorstep. She looks jolly enough, with her toothy smile, though she raises her eyebrows to indicate she heard him. 'Hello, Elspeth, isn't it? I thought I'd call in and see how your father's doing.' She is already in the hallway. 'Were you just going out?'

The fog is now so thick that Elspeth can't see the gate. She takes off her coat, and follows the nurse into the living room. Her father seems to have tried to get up, dislodging the tray and spilling the soup down his trousers.

'Well, now Mr Tunnicliffe, what have you done to yourself?'

As she picks up the fallen bowl beside his chair, Elspeth's nostrils recoil at the unmistakeable stench. She takes the tray into the kitchen, bringing back a dishcloth. The nurse is holding her father's wrist, looking at a mark, a brown circle with ragged edges. Elspeth recognises the shape, it matches the one on her elbow. Her father looks around the nurse, raises one eyebrow and smirks.

She is out of the door, and walking, her footsteps muffled by the fog, down, down to the park, along the path beside the river. Stepping off the path, walking between the trees, she comes to a kind of clearing. The fog is thicker here, she can't see more than a yard or so and, when she looks behind her, there is just a short line of silvery footsteps following her through the grass. But her head is full of fog, too, so she can neither see nor think clearly. She closes her eyes, turns around. The footsteps have disappeared. Which way did she come? Is that a dog barking? She walks forward, meets a bush. Turns. Walks through grass, getting longer, going on and on. There's a fallen down wall, and she sits on a large flat stone, looking around, thinking, I've been here before. She feels dizzy as the familiar whooshing sound of blood pumps through her head. It's sleep, trying to catch her out, but it's so hard to stay awake, easier just to lean here and close her eyes…

There's something wet on her face. Sticky. Heavy breathing. Deep brown eyes. It's a dog, looking at her with his head on one side. He reminds her of the social worker. She giggles.

A voice nearby calls, 'Tinker, come on boy–' and a figure comes out of the fog, like a shadow. 'Hello? Are you all right, love? Are you hurt?'

She puts a hand to her head and realises her hair is wet and tangled, and as she stands she sees mud and grass on her coat. Her shoes and the bottom of her trousers are saturated. She must look a sight, sleeping on the grass, giggling like an idiot. She straightens her shoulders. 'I'm fine, thank you.' With her hands, she brushes herself down. 'Sat down for a rest while I was out walking. Must have dropped off.'

'Don't I know you?' he's looking closely at her. She studies his bald head, his kindly, ruddy face, his paunch, thinking that he does look familiar, perhaps he works at the butcher's. 'It's Elspeth Tunnicliffe isn't it?' When she frowns, he points at his chest, as if she could think he meant someone else, 'Colin. Colin Newbould.'

'I – I – must go. Sorry. Thank you for – for the dog.' That sounds stupid, but she needs to get away. She turns, stumbles. He catches her by the elbow. 'Ouch,' she pulls her arm away from him. 'Sorry, it's just – I hurt my elbow.'

'Don't dash off.' He's smiling.

If she ever thought about seeing him again, and she had, often, it hadn't been a smiling Colin. No, she wouldn't have expected him to be so – well, so friendly.

'You look frozen. The park café is open, they have soup and hot drinks and it'll be warm, and – oh, I'm sorry, I'm gabbling. Anyway, coffee?'

She finds herself walking beside him. They are a few feet from the path, that's all, and on the other side of the trees, across a little bridge over the river, is the old tin tabernacle. She remembers a run-down shell of a building. As fast as anyone tried to turn it into something – a community centre, a shop – it was vandalised. The building that appears from the fog is painted bright blue, with yellow gingham curtains, and as they step inside, she feels the warmth of the wall heaters. They sit at a scrubbed pine table, and while Colin goes to the counter and orders drinks, she strokes Tinker, who has put his head in her lap. The windows are steamed up and running with water.

Colin pulls out a chair. 'You've made a friend there. He doesn't like everybody, you're highly honoured. How long have you been back?'

She tells him she's here temporarily, looking after her father.

'I never thought I'd see you again, not here, anyroad. I was glad you'd got away, didn't think you'd come back.'

So many questions, so many years. She must ask. 'Why?'

'Why what?'

'You dropped me.'

'I dropped you? No, that's not what happened.' He looked shocked.

'Here you are love, that'll warm you through.'

She lifts the glass of mulled wine to her lips, but the steamy sweet aroma is something else, making her pause and frown.

She catches his eye. He's worried. 'Is that still your favourite?' Of course, it's hot Vimto. And it comes back to her. A different café. A glass of steaming Vimto. He grabbed her elbow, pulled her out of the door, along the street, into the house, up the stairs...

'I came round,' Colin says. 'Every day for a week. He told me you didn't want to see me. Then he said you'd gone off with somebody else?'

'No, there was nobody else.'

'I should have been more persistent. I should have known he was lying. I'm sorry. We all knew he led you a dog's life.' Tinker yawns and looks up at her. 'Not like your life,' Colin laughs, and ruffles the dog's ears. 'You live a human's life.'

She looks down at her hands resting in her lap. As they warm, the blister starts to weep. She dabs at it with a napkin, feeling his eyes on her.

'Martini Girl,' she says.

'Yes,' says Colin. 'We knew it wasn't true. Not

then, but later, and then it was too late, you'd gone.'

As he dragged her out of the café, he said to Colin, but so that everybody could hear, 'Nobody wants this one, Martini Girl – anytime, anyplace, that's her. Like mother like daughter.'

She was too embarrassed to go back to college. The bruises took weeks to fade. The first time she went out, it was with whatever she could carry in that little suitcase.

They drink in silence for a few moments, then he says, 'We often talked about you. Wondered what had happened to you, if you were okay, you do hear things–'

'We?'

'Me and Jane. We got married. We've got five kids, six grandkids.' The smile drops off his face and he blushes and stutters, 'Sorry, did you think–'

She sees that this kindly man with the paunch thinks she might still have designs on him, and wants to laugh, but realises she's being unkind, and smiles at him. 'No, that's lovely, I was just thinking – well, that you've done so much with your life, and me, I've done nothing' – except keep running – 'Tell me about your family.'

As she listens to his soft northern burr talking of growing vegetables, of Saturday football and Sunday roasts, and sips the sugary, warm liquid, she feels a melt beginning in her chest, moving through her body; something flinty that has been part of her for so very long, yields, then fades away, allowing her ribs to open and spread, so that she can breathe.

'Thank you,' she says.

As Elspeth reaches the front door, a car pulls into the kerb. The social worker gets out.

'Elspeth, we need to talk, we had another call.'

'Wait there a minute.' She goes into the house, and up the stairs. Her father's voice follows her into the bedroom; he bangs on the ceiling with his walking stick, and is standing at the living room door as she comes down with her holdall. He is still shouting when she closes the door behind her. She hands the keys to the social worker and keeps walking.

Class of '89

I switch on the computer, log in, and that little envelope pops onto the screen. *You've got Mail.* My mouth is dry and my palms begin to itch. It's the first email I've ever received. It can only be from her, of course; I haven't written to anyone else. Amanda Maybury – or *Manda May* as she calls herself these days. She even has her own website – *mandamay.com* – which makes very interesting reading, especially the page about her background. That's not quite how I remember it, Amanda.

My mobile phone rings. It's Brenda. If I don't answer it, she'll report back and I'll get into trouble.

'Where are you?'

'Having coffee.' That much is true. I don't say it's an internet café. She wouldn't expect me to know what one of those is. And I didn't, until a few weeks ago. I saw the poster at the library, for a course called *First Click* and I enrolled for it. I didn't tell Brenda. And if she knew that I'd found out, on the course, about how to use the internet to trace people, she'd have me back there in two shakes. There's a lot I don't tell Brenda. She likes to think we have trust – *rapport,* she calls it – and I go along with her. 'A trouble shared is a trouble halved,' is something she often says. She talks a lot in clichés. In my experience, it's more like 'a trouble shared is trouble doubled'. They write it down and want to talk about it for months.

I read Amanda's email while Brenda talks:

Hey there Jules, Got your friend request via schoolreunion.com. I'm based in the US of A these days, making a modest living in the world of words. How's it going with you? Tell all!! Manda XXX.

As though nothing ever happened. Well, if that's the way she wants to play it, I can manage that.

Brenda says, 'Are you still there, Julie?'

I cut the call. Brenda gave me this mobile so she can keep in touch, but she'll believe me if I say I don't understand how to work it. She's not the brightest button in the box, as my mother used to say – she was another one who talked in clichés – and she'll believe most things I tell her. This internet café is two buses away from the Centre, so there's no risk of running into Brenda or any of the other nurses. It's called *Refresh*. That's a pun. See, I do have a sense of humour, despite what they say. It's important to have a place where I don't need to worry about being watched and talked about, written about, where I can have some privacy.

I read the email again. You'd think we were the greatest of pals. And we were, once, a long time ago. Right from reception class, we were always together. I got my mother to buy me clothes like Amanda's, had my hair cut the same. Like peas in a pod, people used to say. 'Where's your little shadow?' they'd ask if I was out alone. We enjoyed confusing the teachers, pretending to be one another. One day, in sewing class, we hid under the table and I showed her how we could use the needles to prick the tips of our middle fingers. She shouted, 'oww!' but nobody heard. When we pressed our fingers together, mixing our bright red blood, I felt a tingle all the way down to my toes. Then we sucked our fingers and said 'yuk!' and stuck our tongues out at the taste, like sucking pennies, and stared into one another's eyes, and whispered, '*Together, forever*'.

We passed our eleven plus and went to Grammar School together. That's when she started to forget. She made friends with other girls, who took her away from me. She pretended not to remember our promise to one another. Said I was 'cramping her style'. She said, 'stop stalking me'. But we were soulmates.

Years later, when I was in there, I heard a song, and I knew it was our song, that she'd put on the radio, that she was sending a message to me. *You are my soulmate,* it said, *now and forever, two hearts beating as one.* So, I stopped telling them there was nothing the matter with me, and agreed to everything they said, did whatever they wanted, so that I could get out, and find her. That poster in the library was another message from her. *Get on the internet and you'll find me.* And here she is.

I don't reply straight away. I log off, because it's charged by the minute, and order a coffee. When I first came to *Café Refresh*, I didn't recognize all the coffees – latte, macchiato, espresso. Cappuccino – that's the only one I knew, but I've experimented with the others, since. Today, to give me time to think, I treat myself to a panino. They insist on calling it a panini but I did Italian for GCSE and I know it's one panino, two panini. I don't say anything. I don't want to draw attention to myself, be someone they remember. While I eat, I think carefully about what to say to her. Be lighthearted. Don't mention where I've been, it might upset her. On the internet course, I learned about 'profiles' – that's what they call it on in social media – and I put one on *schoolreunion.com*. All I had to do was think about the life that I might have had if… and write it down. Within a few minutes, I'd become a career woman, working in the City, something in investments – keeping it vague – with a penthouse suite. Dropping a trail of breadcrumbs that would bring Amanda back to me. And see, it worked. I don't want to frighten her away.

I finish my panino, log on again, and write the email:

Hello Amanda. Lovely to hear from you. I too am doing quite well for myself as you will see from my profile. May I take this opportunity to congratulate you on the new book? I have read all your books and enjoyed them immensely. Best wishes, Julie.

I'm used to marking time, but this has been one of the longest weeks of my life. I keep my appointment with Brenda and go to the Centre and sit through those interminable group sessions with people who don't give a thought for anyone else. Eventually it's Saturday and I go to *Café Refresh*. And sure enough, there's an email. I can read her mid-Atlantic drawl in the words. Real Americans probably don't talk like this:

Gee, Ju-ju, you're living it up in the Smoke? So glad you're well again. I had been poorly recently, but how did she know? *I'll be in the UK next month to launch the book.* I know that; her schedule is on her website. *Maybe we could catch lunch?*

I can hardly believe it's that easy. After all the waiting, the time has come. I know all about her wonderful career. *My* career, stolen from *me*. I sometimes wonder whether that day, under the table in sewing class, we changed clothes to fool the teachers and forgot to change back. That bestselling author with the glittering lifestyle? It should be *me*. I stare at the email so hard my eyes go out of focus. I scratch my palms, remembering.

My parents believed the official version: Amanda's version. They said they didn't know how they could live with the shame. Well, they didn't need to, for very long. I was three streets away, on an early morning cycle ride, when I heard the explosion and looked behind me to see an enormous ball of orange flame leaping above the rooftops. I cycled home as fast as I could. At first, I thought I'd taken a wrong turning, for one side of the house was missing. Where the kitchen, and my parents' bedroom above, should have been, there was a pile of black, smoking bricks. The lawn was covered in shards of glass and charred wood, mixed with pieces of fabric. The window of the lounge had blown out but I could see, on the mantelpiece, my father's collection of toby jugs. That's when I screamed. The neighbours stood in a crowd, not speaking, just staring at me. When the fire brigade arrived along with an ambulance, they wrapped me in a blanket; for shock, they said, and gave me a hot drink. It was a shock. I had nowhere to go as my grandmother said she couldn't cope with me, and she was right, because she became ill shortly afterwards and had to go into hospital. But the police, and the coroner, they believed me; they called it a tragic accident. They said they thought mother would have come downstairs to make tea; Dad was probably having a lie-in. If she smelt the gas as she went into the kitchen, it would have been too late: she switched on the kitchen light.

You might say that as well as stealing my future, Amanda stole my past. See what she made me do. My parents were everything I had.

I walk around the block to think things through. When I come back, someone is in my place, but I keep calm, stand beside him, waiting patiently for him to finish, which he does quite quickly, and then I log on to my email and send a reply:

Do confirm your London dates and I'll ask my PA to check my availability.

The PA is a nice touch, I think; I got the idea from two women I overheard in the café, talking about their office. As I hit 'send', I realize I must have been holding my breath for I feel quite faint. I inhale slowly through my nose and count to ten while I exhale through my mouth, like Brenda showed me.

This week, I take my scrapbook to the Centre and work on it; I want it to be perfect for Amanda.

Brenda says, 'That's good progress, Julie, it could be very good for you, putting your life story together, getting everything into perspective.'

She even helps me find all the newspaper articles. First, my parents' accident. I give her the date and Brenda looks it up on the computer in the office. She's one of those one-fingered people, banging away at the keyboard, and I have to restrain myself from pushing her away and doing it myself. She prints off the article about the fire.

'Gosh, Julie, that must have been so traumatic for you. No wonder…'

I nod, and look sad.

Next, she finds the story about Reggie Price. It even mentions Amanda, the reporter on the local paper, who found the crucial bit of evidence that convicted him. Reggie lived near us, with his elderly mother; he had what they call learning difficulties these days. According to this article, he's still serving a life sentence for murdering that woman in the park. Poor Reggie; they say his mother's last words were that he'd told the truth, he'd been at home with her. The Chief Constable gave Amanda an award. It was *my* award of course; she couldn't have done it without me. Amanda never admitted that an anonymous letter had led her to find Reggie's scarf near the murder scene; it was nothing to do with her investigative skills. What would happen if I told them that Reggie had been exactly where his mother said he was? And that Reggie, always eager to help, had lent me his scarf earlier that day?

Next, Brenda finds the article in the local paper about Amanda's mother, who was a bigshot in the local WI, so it's quite a big piece, and it says how proud she was of her only daughter. I remember the day I met her in the shopping mall and had to listen while she went on and on about her brilliant daughter.

'And what are you doing these days, Julie?' she asked.

She knew very well that I was working in a factory, in the only job in that would have me without a school reference. Only minutes later, she tripped and fell down the escalator in Lewis's; she was in a coma for months with a head injury. I don't think Amanda ever knew that I was the last person to speak to her mother.

I visited her in the hospital on the very day she died.

Reggie Price was Amanda's lucky break. A job in London, on a national newspaper, and then somebody gave her the idea of writing a series of novels featuring a journalist who investigated crimes. I had to give up my job and my little bedsit to be near her. Once more, I gave up everything for her. I did it willingly, though, because with my family all gone, she was all I had. While my savings lasted, I was with her every day, everywhere: on the underground, in the shops, at the theatre. Even when she was at home, I was never far away.

She wrote a novel, *Stalked,* and sold the film rights in America for an astronomical sum. Off she went to the States, to be 'consultant' to the film company. The next thing I heard, she'd married Max, the producer. All without a backward glance to the person who had made it possible. Me. But then, I became too busy to keep in touch with Amanda. It was only recently, through the internet, that I found her again.

Tuesday comes round at last, and as soon as I

switch on the computer, there's the little envelope and Amanda's reply:

Hey kid! As though I'm that six-year-old again, having a bubble-gum blowing contest with her. *Hey kid! It's great that we can put our little contretemps behind us.* Little contretemps? That's hardly what I'd call her theft of my work and my life. *I arrive in London on 3rd. There's a book signing the following day – 6pm at Bookenz. Could your PA fix us up with a restaurant?* A restaurant? What kind of lifestyle does she think I can afford? One visit a week to *Café Refresh* and the bus fare to Brenda's office uses all my spare cash. Though of course, she never did think about me; isn't that the point? I look down at my hands, willing my fingers to stop scratching my palms so that I can use the keyboard.

I worked for months on my A Level psychology essay: *Nature v Nurture – can sociopathy in childhood be cured?* – just to receive a curt note from the head teacher: 'Disqualified for cheating'. He said I'd 'tarnished the school's reputation' and expelled me without finishing my A levels. Then, the final humiliation – I heard that Amanda got an A Star for her essay, and was nominated for *The Herald* Young Journalist Trophy. Which meant a journalism traineeship. When it was published in *The Herald,* I found it was *my* essay.

Even then, I believed our childhood promise: 'Together, forever'. I'd have followed her anywhere, done anything. I typed:

Dear Amanda, Why not eat at mine? I found a recipe for Creole Fish Stew in the Sunday supplement which I'm keen to try. It was in the same edition as a special offer for French kitchen knives, superb quality and guaranteed for life.

There is pink champagne in flutes, canapés and petit fours. I watch you scan the audience and then shrug, possibly because you think I haven't come. You've forgotten how we used to play with disguises. We still share many physical attributes, just as we did as children. Same shape face, same height. There's no grey in your hair, though, it's curly and glossy, which is not natural, I think, but it's a similar length to mine if I untie my pony-tail. As you move around the rostrum, reading, gesturing, the layers of silk fall perfectly, draping your well-toned, well-fed figure. I can see you are the product of an expensive diet and a fitness regime. My body on the other hand is the by-product of a stodgy, institutional diet. But these are trivial differences that can easily be remedied by stylists and personal trainers. We still like similar colours: purple, violet, indigo. I think how well you will coordinate with my window boxes. Just this morning, I noticed the crocuses pushing their sharp green spears through the moist compost. In the next few months, iris and delphinium will bloom on my little balcony high above the hustle and bustle of London. It will be the perfect setting for you.

While you sign books, chat with the people, laugh as they compliment you, I take off my hat and coat and watch you notice me, the last person in the queue. You frown, look again, then smile and come forward, wrapping me in a cloud of Chanel. 'Ju-ju' you say, 'Is it really you?'

Why did you use my childhood nickname? It only emphasized how much you have betrayed me; and air-kissing in that pseudo-celebrity fashion – mwah, mwah;

and when you looked me up and down, I felt you judging, criticising. You said goodbye to your agent and we left. I even paid for a taxi, to be sure of it. As we climbed the four flights of stairs to my little studio flat, you said, 'Jeez, is there no elevator?' At the top, you stopped and stared around with – yes, pity in your eyes. And when I showed you my scrapbook, my – no, our life story, you tossed your hair, and laughed. Following pity with humiliation. You left me with no choice.

When you tasted the wine, you wrinkled that pretty little nose and picked up the bottle to check the label. Yes, it was the best New Zealand Pinot Grigio; but with a month's supply of tranylcypromine ground into it. I pretended I'd lost my prescription, and as usual, Brenda believed me. I'd done my research, on the internet. I knew how much was enough to make you listen without interrupting. I told you what I wanted, just you and I, one soul, one life. Even though you couldn't move a muscle by then, I saw it in your eyes – the same look of disbelief I'd seen in the eyes of the teachers, and my parents, over twenty years ago, and on the faces of all those doctors and social workers. Even then, a few well-chosen words could have ended it differently. Though I suppose you had trouble speaking by then. I didn't think of that. Luckily, the knives were just as advertised.

I've invested in several more window boxes and a nice wooden planter. Carrying all that compost up four flights of stairs was quite an effort, I can tell you. There was a sharp downpour yesterday and a faint hint of Chanel wafted through the open window. When I looked out, I thought I saw a flash of violet silk between the petunias. I became very excited, anticipating those long summer nights, sitting on my balcony, writing my next novel, with you. Two hearts, beating as one.

I've bought a home computer now, so I don't need to go out much. I'm very busy. There's a lot of correspondence to deal with. Today I send two emails. The first, to Max:

I'm not coming back. I've decided to stay with my oldest friend, in London.

If he doesn't believe me, and tries to visit, I can deal with that. The second email is to Will Staunton, who was part of our circle in the sixth form:

Hey Will, I got your friend request via schoolreunion.com. I'm in the UK, looking up old pals. You were such a mate when I had that trouble back in Sixth Form. Remember how Julie pretended to have written that essay! Deluded or what?? I want to show my gratitude to all the folk who rooted for me back then. Any chance of meeting up? Manda XX

I'm pushing a few forget-me-not seeds into the window boxes when the doorbell rings. Brenda calls through the intercom, 'Julie, you haven't collected your prescription.' I explain – again – that Julie has gone and left no forwarding address.

Joyriding

I'm already awake when I hear Mum come in but I keep my eyes closed so she can't ask me nothing then I don't have to lie to her face. Don't be late for school, love, off to see your brother. It's Wednesday so she'll be with Jack all day. She's done a rota for the other days so she can go to work and pay the bills. Monday's Gran, Tuesdays Auntie Lynne, Jamie gets Thursdays off college specially, Friday it's Dad in the mornings because he can't get much time off work even though Mum says he could if he wanted, then I take over from him because school agreed to call it study time. Everybody's in and out all weekend. Mum's there every night after work until ten. She'd stay all night if she didn't have to look after me and Jamie. Sometimes I wish she would stay. When she's here, she just stresses about homework, and bangs round washing and ironing, then she's bawling her eyes out and blowing her nose on one of Jack's tee-shirts, gross.

—

I text Layla and when Mum's car's driven off I get up. I'm literally bricking it, thinking what if I get caught. My fingers are slippery on my buttons. Jamie shouts me to hurry up and I'm like, you think you're the boss of me just cos Mum's not here? He thinks he's too special to get his own breakfast. I don't say any of that cos he'll grass me up if he twigs I'm bunking off.

Layla's mum's at work so we can change out of our uniforms and put our makeup on at hers and she says I look about 19 and I'm like so do you, then we go for the train. They've moved Ethan to near York but he says there's a train station and we can walk from there. About twenty times I check the visiting order that Layla's printed off. It'll be the first time I've seen him since. He's written, I've written back and his writing's better. He says he has to go to classes because he didn't go to school much, before, and he likes it, he's thinking about going to college when he comes out.

I know all the stops to York from coming here with Mum and Dad for Christmas shopping and stuff. Last year we came to the panto and Jack went on about how this crap was for kids and he'd rather be out with his mate Ethan and Mum said, make an effort, for the family. There's a big poster on the platform for Jack and the Beanstalk, and that makes me tear up, cos I want to hear Jack banging on again.

After we change trains in York I feel proper scared and my nail art's gone soggy round the edges from me chewing and Layla laughs and I'm like it's all right for you, if my Mum found out she'd skin me alive. Outside the station we ask the way and suddenly there's this giant fence with barbed wire on top and HMYOI across the front. A guard checks my visiting order and makes us put our phones in a locker. Nobody checks our age. A guard takes us to a building that looks like the health centre, and we wait in a lobby, exactly like waiting at the doctor's. After a bit, the guard comes back holding a bunch of keys that are attached to her with a chain and she calls our names and we follow her down a corridor into this big room that looks like the school canteen.

There's a row of boys sitting at tables, with their backs

to the wall, all wearing grey jumpers. I'm looking round for a skinhead, then a boy waves and it's Ethan, but with his hair grown, it's blond, I didn't know that, he looks different, softer. He nods, alright? I sit down and look at him and look away because I can't get how he's the same but not the same. He's had his teeth fixed from the accident. Last time I saw him was in hospital with the police taking him away. Mum and Dad saw him in Court but I wasn't allowed. He smells like soap. He's chunkier as well. His mum and dad never fed him proper and he used to eat at ours after he was friends with Jack.

Layla says, I'll get us some teas, and heads off to a hatch next to the kids play area. I look at him and he looks at me, and his face is pink and I feel hot and red. He says, I've got me date. What? Tagging. What's that? I get out early with a tag that goes round me ankle, I have to live at me Dad's and have a curfew. Three weeks, on Christmas Eve.

He got two years for stealing the car and dangerous driving, how come he's out in three weeks? You can't come home, Jamie and his mates, they'll kill you. He looks tragic, tearing up, then he makes a pfff noise with his teeth between his lips, like the old Ethan, not scared of nobody. Layla puts the teas down and goes back for hers, then stands watching the kids playing. I'm like, can't you live somewhere else? He shakes his head. I'm bricking it but I know he's going to ask and then he does. What about us, are we sound? Are we still going out? I think what if Mum and Dad found out, and Jamie, he'd probably kill me as well, but if I finish with Ethan, I'll lose them anyway. So I nod. He smiles then. His new teeth are nice. It's not your way of telling me to get lost, then? No, Ethan, really, listen, Jamie'll kill you for what you did to Jack. He pulls his head back until his eyes are little slits. What I did to Jack?

I was scared when Jack brought him home first. He stood in the hallway, looking round him, and saw me peeking through the banisters, and stared at me with these little slitty eyes and his lip curled. I was literally goose flesh all over. Everybody knew Ethan's rep. Jack and Jamie fell out. They'd been twins all the way, they did the same and talked the same, and there was times even I couldn't tell which was which. But then Jack started hanging with Ethan, and Jamie was like a bear with a headache. Mum tried to talk sense to him, but Dad said it was good, that the twins needed to separate, find themselves as individuals. Mum threw that back at him, after the accident. It was one of the reasons Dad left. I was glad Jamie was friends with Ethan because when the twins weren't taken up with each other, they both had time for me. And it was exciting, when Jack and Ethan let me and Layla go with them. Layla and Jack, me and Ethan. After the accident, everybody said Ethan had always been bad news, he was a bad influence on Jack.

Layla's back. She sits down, says carry on I won't listen. He says, how's Jack doing? I'm like the doctors want to switch him off and Mum won't allow it, she thinks he'll come round one day. That was another reason Dad left, because he said they should let the doctors switch Jack off. Ethan says, you hear about things like that, she's right to wait, I would.

The guard says finish your visits please. Ethan leans

towards me and the guard says no contact and inside, I'm glad. He wants me to send him some truck magazines. Mr Pradesh in the newsagent's will tell me what he means. I turn round at the door, he's biting his fingernails, looking at the table.

The connecting train from York is cancelled so we're late and Mum texts me where am I because Jamie's texted her that I'm not back from school. He'll be wanting me to cook his tea. I text her that I'm having tea at Layla's.

Friday, I go to the hospital at dinner break. Since Dad moved in with Gran, Friday's pretty much the only time I see him. Sometimes we go to the canteen for egg and chips. We have a laugh. It sounds cruel, but we forget, for a few minutes. I don't tell Mum because she'd stress at there being nobody with Jack, even though it's only half an hour and if he hasn't woken up for eight months he's not going to do it then, is he?

Mum and Dad are by Jack's bed, talking. Dad sees me and comes out. We've had some news, from the victim service, about Ethan, he's getting out in a few weeks. We can't face it, seeing him around. He won't be allowed to approach us, but even so. I'm going home now, to break it to Jamie. Mum's holding Jack's hand. She's thin, like dried out, no crying left.

Driving home, I keep my lips closed because stuff about Ethan is trying to burst out of me. Dad says, I know love, you're as shocked as we are. We sit in the car outside our house, looking through the windscreen. The Santa on the Wilkinson's chimney is hanging sideways. The drizzle makes it nearly dark and the lights on the houses look blurry and sad, like they're crying. Dad says, shall I come round and put the lights up? I shrug. I don't want to think about Christmas.

Jamie's in his room. Dad goes in and shuts the door. I put a couple of pizzas in the oven with some chips and get the ketchup out of the fridge then Jamie screams I'll kill him, I swear, and the bottle slips out of my fingers and I watch it smash and splash giant red splotches across the floor. Jamie runs downstairs and slams out of the house. He'll be going to his mates. I know what they'll be talking about. Dad hugs me. I know you're upset, love, aren't we all.

Saturday, Layla texts me to go round, she's got a letter off Ethan. He says, dont worry, I wont tell but I havnt got nobody and if I cant come home yu have to come wiv me. Iv got a mate here from Belfast says I can get a job there. I dont care ware so long as ur there.

It's a bit exciting, thinking about running away. Belfast sounds boring, though. Once, Mum and Dad took me and the twins to Tenerife. That was mega. I can pass for older and we could get jobs in a bar. Would you come? and Layla says, and be gooseberry to you two? Which makes us both think of Jack, who she fancied like mad, before, and we go quiet.

Then she says, tell your mum and dad, you've got to. I know. Before I leave hers, we tear Ethan's letters into little bits. It's pouring freezing rain. I get to the hospital drenched, my shoes are squelching and my hair's sticking to my face, and when Mum sees me looking through the window, she jumps up and runs out. Jesus, you look like a ghost, and puts her hand over her mouth because she's not supposed to say things like that. The nurse brings a towel and Mum rubs my hair like a little kid and I put on her fleecy onesie that she keeps at the hospital just in case. I'm crying and she hugs me like she hasn't since that night. She says, I'll get you a hot chocolate, warm you through. I sit down and hold Jack's hand, thinking he might wake up and say, don't be soppy. It's the first time we've been on our own since.

Why, just why didn't you put your seatbelt on? You went on and on about thieving a car. I know how you felt, I felt the same round Ethan, excited, dangerous. You knew he didn't want to because he was on a caution and he promised, if I went out with him, he'd go straight. But you kept on til he showed you how to start the car with a wire. He wanted to go home then. I made him get in. Layla was with us because she fancied you. You was literally driving like a maniac, buzzing with the skunk. So I made you get in the passenger seat. You told me how to drive. But just why didn't you put your seat belt on? My fingerprints must've been on the steering wheel, but they didn't look because Ethan owned up straight away. They believed me. And Ethan, when he swapped seats with me, and I said I'd stick by him, he believed me. But I can't.

Mum's pushing a paper cup into my hands, wrapping my fingers into the warm chocolatey cream that's running over the side. You can't change your story now, love. It won't help Jack. Leave it be.

Under Pressure

Well, there we have it: the letter has been signed and is winging its way to Brussels. I turn the radio off and look out of the window. The sun has gone behind a cloud and it's starting to rain. Below me, a couple of hardy souls in short sleeves are braving the Promenade. A few months ago, I expected to be celebrating this historic moment, but now…

Barbara taps me on the arm. 'Look at this one, Harry, it's lovely. Three bedrooms, large, mature gardens—'

Pushing my chair back and standing up, I accidentally knock against her. 'We only need one bedroom. There's no point having a family house when that family lives on the other side of the world.'

In three steps I'm at the door, reaching for my coat. A quick walk on the Prom should clear my head. As I close the door, I glimpse her half smile, half frown, and wonder briefly why she's sitting on the floor.

The wind bites straight through my overcoat and I'm shivering in no time, so I stand in one of the shelters, watching the rain sweeping in from the sea. Grey and dreary. It suits my mood. I feel such a fool, but Barbara is the last person I can talk to about it.

There is the most awful smell. I look round to find an elderly gentleman – if I can use that term – stretched out along the bench. Which is why I never sit down in these shelters. I pull my collar up against the wind, and stride out hard and fast towards the Pier.

No matter how it works out, it's going to be too late for me. Take back economic control, they said. Too much regulation from Brussels. Hah! How we cheered, that morning. How we laughed at the sour grapes lot, banging on about a second referendum, accusing us of ruining the futures of our children, when of course the opposite was true. We did it for our grandchildren's future, and, if it comes to it, for the future of the country. All they seem to care about, these youngsters who go on about Europe, is gay politics and cheap travel. And, don't get me started on the fuzzy wuzzy

Guardian-reading liberals who latch on to any feel-good idea that happens to be in fashion.

The rain is bucketing down, running from my trousers into my shoes, so I turn at the Pier and make my way back to the hotel. As I'm shaking my coat out in the foyer, Simon, I think his name is, comes out of the manager's office.

'Mr Keale. Could I have a word–'

'As you can see, I'm drenched; I need to get into some dry clothes.'

'Of course. If you could call down later, to discuss the bill?'

With a flick of my hand in acknowledgement, I head for the lift. As it rises to the third floor, I feel my spirits sinking further, if that's possible, at the mental picture of Barbara. Sure enough, I open the door to meet her sad, brown eyes, like an abandoned puppy's, waiting for me. I know she isn't happy, and I have only myself to blame. Instead of the lopsided grin, and the cheeky twinkle in her eyes that used to light up her face, she frowns so much these days that she's developed a deep crease between her eyebrows. That crease is a judgement, a criticism that follows me around the room like one of those portraits that people talk about.

She jumps up. 'Harry, you're wet through,' and goes into the bathroom, coming out with a couple of thin, grey towels. She rubs one between her fingers. 'We could bring our own towels out of storage, Harry. But there's nowhere to wash and dry them'. You see, she turns everything into a reminder of my failures.

I decide to make an effort. 'Come on, old fruit, what's for lunch?' and her face lifts immediately. As I change into dry clothes and hang my wet things on the shower rail in the bathroom, she buzzes about in the kitchenette, and produces a bowl of rather watery looking soup and a thin slice of white bread.

I peer into the bowl. 'What flavour is this?'

She decides I'm criticizing. 'If you'd let me do the shopping,' – she speaks in that plaintive voice that she's developed lately – 'or at least go with you, I might be able to pick up some tastier snacks.'

The frown, with its ugly crease, is back. I fight an urge to throw the soup across the room. I've always prided myself on being an even-tempered chap, so I hold one hand still with the other and say, 'It's lovely, dear, I was only going to suggest we make a note of the brand.'

That shuts her up, but only for a few minutes. No sooner have I pushed my bowl away than she puts the iPad in front of me and points at the photograph of a detached house. It looks pretty much the same as the one we left. There it is again, that feeling of being literally hot under the collar. I run a finger round my neck to loosen it.

It's the thin-lipped smile, and that voice, an octave too high. 'What about this one, Harry? Two bedrooms, quite a small garden, and a workshop where you could do your carpentry. You always said you'd have more time for your carpentry when you retired.'

'That's a nice thought, old thing, but I packed up my carpentry tools and sent them to George, remember?' When our grandson visited from New Zealand last year, he showed a great interest in woodwork and I wanted to encourage him.

'No, I didn't.'

'Didn't what?'

'I'm sorry, I didn't mention it, but Andrea said George was more interested in computers these days and not to bother sending the tools.'

I'm torn between irritation that she made this decision without consulting me, and a wave of pleasure at discovering that I still have my tools. That carpentry set was a gift from my late father when I completed my apprenticeship. I kept it for sentimental reasons, even though I never went back to carpentry after I set up the fitted kitchen business; but, as Barbara says, I often talked about rekindling the old skills when I retired. She's watching me. To avoid that ugly crease, I smile. 'I'm pleased. Maybe the boy will do some carpentry with me, when he visits us next.'

Emboldened, I suppose, by my good humour, she pulls her chair up to mine and leans against me, tapping away on the iPad, chattering away. 'We've been here for almost three months. I know you're disappointed about Adelaide Close falling through, but we do need to move quickly so our money in the bank doesn't lose its value.'

She knows nothing about financial

management. She's parroting what she's heard me say in the past. It makes me wonder whether she's being sarcastic; whether she's guessed. I loosen my tie, and open the top button of my shirt. So far as Barbara is concerned, the house in Adelaide Close was withdrawn from the market the day before we were due to move in. Our own home had sold. So we had to move into this little hotel, temporarily, while we found another house. Give Barbara her due, she took it well. Sorted out a few things and sent the rest off to a storage unit. What I didn't tell her was that there never was a new home. Nor is there the money to buy one. The proceeds from our house sale went straight to the liquidators. I was certain I'd find a way around it. Surely, they'd allow me to keep our home? No, it turns out I'd guaranteed a business loan with it, years ago. Everything went – even the investments that were supposed to provide me with a very decent pension – all gone.

Which means, of course, that I can't tell her how little we have left, and even this will run out completely within days. She has absolutely no idea of the pressure I've been under, the lengths I've gone to, trying to save our house and our savings. She sits beside me, chattering on, prodding at the iPad, bringing up more photographs of houses for sale, pointing out this and that for my inspection, until I feel I'm going to burst. To calm myself, I turn to look out of the window, though I can see nothing for the rain battering against the glass.

There's a knock at the door and that manager chap, Sean, I think he's called, says, 'Mr Keale? Could I have a word?'

'I'll be down shortly,' I say. I can hear him shuffling his feet outside the door for a few moments – that's how thin the door is – before he goes away.

'Is something wrong, Harry?'

How I despise that lipstick stain on her teeth. Why can she not understand how difficult all this is, for me? The smile drops from her face and her bottom lip starts to quiver. For goodness' sake. She knows I hate blubbering, so she walks into the little kitchenette and washes the pots, with her back to me. The sun comes out briefly and for a while I watch a woman on the beach, throwing a stick for her dog. This view is so familiar; in the early days of our marriage, we spent holidays here, and they are happy memories. I thought bringing Barbara here would give us both a pleasant break, but it's not working out that way.

'What about Paphos?' She startles me; I didn't hear her approach. 'We could spend some time at the apartment. You need a break, Harry, it's been very stressful, retiring, selling the business, moving house—'

If I have a pet hate, it's my wife trying to read my emotional state. I want to shout, 'There is no bloody apartment in Cyprus. The blasted liquidators froze it along with the rest of our assets.' But I've always been in charge, looked after her, taken care of our finances, and I will sort it out, given time. Again, I wonder if she knows, if she's testing me, trying to make me confess to what an unholy mess I'd made of it all.

'We discussed this,' I say, to wrong-foot her. 'The apartment is let for the season. Don't you remember?'

'If you say so, Harry.' She puts down the tea-towel and picks up the iPad. 'Adelaide Close is back on the market.'

'What makes you think that?'

'Here it is on the agent's listing.'

I don't need to look. They never took the *For Sale* sign down. Blast that iPad. Either I left it unlocked when I went for my walk, or she's discovered the password. 'It must be a mistake, or the estate agent would have been in touch.'

She's looking at the desolate view from the window. Her profile is still striking. It reminds me of that autumn day I came home to find her having tea with her WI friends, holding forth about jam or cakes or whatever it is they do. My Barbara in her element. Over dinner, I told her I'd decided to accept a good offer for the business and retire. She was thrilled. Now look at us, on a rainswept spring day in this shabby seafront hotel, living in a room which gets smaller every time she begs me to bring bits and pieces from the storage unit to cheer the place up. An embroidered table-cloth that we bought the last time we were in Cyprus; a toaster and microwave and china cups and saucers to complement the hotel's sorry supplies; a painting of the two of us by one of those street painters outside the Sacre Coeur.

'Should I ring the estate agent, Harry? If it is back on the market, can't we just buy it? After all, our cash is in the bank, waiting.'

No cash in the bank. Another turn of the screw. My collar is definitely too tight. I point at the iPad. 'Tell you what. The one with the workshop, now you've given me the good news about my carpentry kit, that's not such a bad idea. Why not make an appointment to view?'

She perks up straight away. 'You mean, I can come with you this time?' I give her the mobile phone and within seconds she's chatting away to the estate agent, and announces, 'We can view this afternoon. Can we stay in town for a cream tea afterwards?'

Give her an inch and she takes a mile. 'Maybe another time, sweetheart.' I pat my stomach. 'Still need to shed a few pounds.' She flushes, embarrassed that she's forgotten about my diet. The real reason of course is that I need to watch the pennies, not the pounds.

On our way through the lobby, my name is called, and before I can get to the door, Barbara stops and says, 'Hello', and there's Sid again.

He holds out a hand to Barbara. 'Mrs Keale? I do hope you're feeling better. Your husband said you've been unwell?'

She looks puzzled. I've told her not to answer the door if I'm out, and I always collect the mail from the night porter. From behind her, I purse my mouth and give him a little shake of the head, and he has the grace to blush.

I hold the door open and Barbara is outside when he says, 'Mr Keale, could I have a word?' He's not going to give up. I close the door between myself and Barbara and turn to him. 'I want to remind you about the bar bill?' Damn, that would be the bottle of wine we had on Barbara's birthday. 'And, about next week.' I'm thinking about next week, too, as the cheque for last week's bill will certainly bounce by then, but he says, 'It's Easter, the start of the season. The hotel is booked solid from Thursday, so...'

Barbara is tugging at the door from outside but I hold it fast. I put my hand up to stop him talking. 'Thank you very much, Steve, is it?' He shrugs. 'It's all in hand. We should be out of your hair very soon.'

'If I can help you to find—'

'Don't trouble yourself.' I sweep out of the door, catching Barbara by the elbow as I go, down the steps and into the car park, looking around. No car. I keep forgetting. I steer her towards the gate. 'Car's not back from repair yet, trouble getting a foreign component.' I lead her across the road to the bus stop. Once things are sorted out, I'll be able to replace the car, like everything else, and she'll be none the wiser.

The property is a poky new-build on a cul-de-sac in the suburbs, the kind of house we lived in when Andrea was a baby. The other five or six that she'd shortlisted since we'd been living in the hotel had proved unsuitable for one reason or another. Of course, I hadn't actually viewed any of them. I spent a couple of hours in the library researching the area, then came home with reasons why they weren't suitable. To be fair, she's taken on board what I said, started looking at smaller houses, and in neighbourhoods she wouldn't have considered, not so long ago.

On the bus back, Barbara taps my arm and

looks hopefully at me. 'What did you think, Harry, really?'

'It's very nice. Yes, I can't think of any…'

'Reason to turn it down?' She laughs, a little too shrilly. Again, that feeling that she has me rumbled. 'You see, Harry, I do listen. We need to downsize, to realize some capital, to bolster up the pension, like you said.'

No capital to realize; no pension to be bolstered. It's a curse and a blessing that Barbara has always been happy to leave the financial side of things to me. It might have helped to share the burden. But I couldn't bear the look of disappointment in her eyes. Hence the retirement story. When I told her, she started to bring home cruise brochures. I told her we'd think about a holiday after the house sale. She hasn't mentioned it lately.

The man in front of us is reading the newspaper. The headlines are more of the same. Gloating. It's as though even he is rubbing my nose in it. Of course, I've only myself to blame for being taken in. We expected things to get a little rocky. Our share prices did a dive. But it settled. Then my German contact, Hans Fluchter, phoned. Sales of my kitchens across Europe had grown my business from a tin shed at the edge of a car park, to a purpose-built factory on the ring road, employing five hundred designers, production staff and fitters. I had a team dedicated to the new German kitchen design.

'It's good news for you, Hans,' I said. 'The euro being so strong means this deal will be twenty percent cheaper.'

But he was calling to pull out. Given there was a lead-in time of two years from design to delivery, he said this was compromised by the Brexit timescale. As no one could guarantee we'd have a trade deal in two years, they would stop now. It turned out the contract was signed but not sealed and there was nothing I could do. We'd invested in the production, so we looked for new markets, and had some interest in Canada but too little too late. Our creditors seemed to sniff trouble and called in the loans. Within two weeks of Hans's phone call, I had nowhere to turn. Twenty years of building up a business, all gone west, as they say. There's been some recovery since, of course; rescue plans and whatnot, and who knows what will happen in the long run, it could all turn around, but it'll be too late for businesses like mine. I was done for in that first dip.

We sold Barbara's little runabout, since we only needed one car, and she doesn't know it but her mother's jewellery came in useful, and one way and another I managed for three months. That's how long it took the liquidators to get a court order for the house. Then we had nothing. I applied for those pension credits, and that was a humiliating malarkey. It came through the other day and I was shocked; it won't pay the rent on anything I'd be prepared to ask Barbara to live in.

While all this is churning around in my mind, Barbara is chattering on, trying to find everything she can that was positive about the dismal little box we viewed. She taps my arm again and while I struggle to control myself, says, 'Can we stop off in town and get a birthday card for Sylvia?'

Damn. My stomach fills with dread as I realize Sylvia will be planning her usual spring birthday ball and may be trying to find our address, to send our invitation. I've managed to avoid friends so far. Watching the rain pouring down the window of the bus, I wonder how I can divert her attention from Sylvia.

'Tell you what, let's have that cream tea. One scone won't hurt the waistline.'

It means stopping off in town, but this resort is a good distance from our village, which is why I chose it of course. I've completely forgotten that Sally Wetherby, one of Barbara's cronies from the WI, retired to the coast a couple of years ago, until we are seated in Bella's Pantry, and there she is. Barbara rushes across before I can stop her. I hear her telling Sally that we are between houses and temporarily staying in a hotel.

Sally says, 'I was so sorry to hear about Harry's business.'

I call Barbara over. Well, it may be more of a shout. She looks a little shocked and so does Sally. 'Sorry, but I left my wallet at the hotel, we need to go.'

Sally says, 'Don't worry, let me,' but I have

Barbara by the elbow and propel her out of the tearoom.

We have a quiet night in, watching television. On every channel, somebody has his or her two-penn'orth to offer about the fact that Brexit has been triggered. I can't concentrate, I'm too rattled by the conversations with Steve, or Simon, and Sally. Six days to go. If Barbara gets wind of just how badly I've let her down, she may leave me. I can't have that. What would she do without me?

As she's getting into bed, she asks again about the house we viewed. I say, 'Let's sleep on it.'

Looking out of the window, I can only differentiate the black sky from the black sea by the line of lights twinkling along the Promenade. I nudge the iPad into life and put in the password. When I put 'houses to let' into the search box, up comes a list of letting agents. Beneath several of these it says, 'You visited this site last week', or 'You visited this site today'. It's as I feared, Barbara has guessed the password and she is ahead of me. I skim through the sites but there's nothing, not even quite a small apartment that my meagre pension credits can afford.

There is one more option. I must take my pride in my hands and phone Andrea. If I can get Ben, my son-in-law, on the phone, have a man to man talk, he might lend me enough to manage, until I get back on my feet. Barbara does this *Face2Face* thing on the iPad, and we talk to Andrea and the children every week, but I'd wake her if I tried it. It's too expensive to call overseas from my mobile phone. I jot down Andrea's number from Barbara's address book and, about four in the morning, slip out.

The rain stops during the two mile walk to the industrial estate where the storage unit is located. I have to wake the security guard as I don't have the swipe card that opens the customer entrance. I count off the rows of green metal containers from A to G, and then count in to the sixth container. When my key slips into the padlock I congratulate myself that I've remembered it correctly. I've created something of a sitting area, with an armchair on a rug, a small bookcase, and a few other bits and pieces which I unpacked. A little sanctuary. The fluorescent strip is rather harsh, but even so, sitting there, I feel immediately calmer. I search through a couple of crates marked 'Harry's shed' and find my carpentry tools, in their original wooden cabinet. There are tears in my eyes as I lay them out on the rug: my folding boxwood rule; a set of chisels; a bradawl; the claw hammer; and my tenon saw, prized for its fine, accurate cut.

I get to the estate agent just at opening time. When I say I'm there to make an offer, the receptionist ushers me into the manager's office. After engaging him for a good ten minutes in discussing the area, the benefits of living in a new-build and the building guarantees, I ask, 'Could I possibly use your phone? Need to move some money about. Cash purchase. Won't take long.'

'Of course.' He gives up his seat. 'Dial nine for an outside line. Shout if you need anything.'

Andrea picks up the phone. My hopes of speaking to Ben are dashed when she says, 'He's in the city, on business. What is it, Dad? Is Mum okay?'

What can I do? I've alerted her now; if I say nothing, she'll be on the *Face2Face* thing to her mother in two shakes. I give her an edited summary.

'But Dad, if you've lost the business, your pension, your investments, and you're homeless, what's going to happen? How's Mum coping?'

'I haven't told your mother.'

'Dad, you are such a plank. She must know something's going on.'

'I assure you she doesn't. And I'd be grateful if you didn't tell her.'

'You have to tell her, Dad. She'll be worried sick.'

'I think I can look after your mother's best interests.'

'Well it's not going well so far, is it, Dad?'

That hurts. I explain that I need a small loan, a couple of thousand, to tide us over, so I can rent a property, and start sorting things out.

'Course we'll help, Dad, but you must tell Mum so we can come up with a plan together.' If Ben was there, he would understand why I can't tell Barbara. 'Don't you think,' Andrea says, when I don't respond, 'all this mess is because you've been keeping secrets from her?'

I think 'secrets' a little unfair; I've only been protecting her mother. The estate agent is peering through the window. I signal five minutes. He nods and goes back to fiddling with the window display.

'What time will Ben be home?'

'It's no use thinking Ben will back you up, Dad. This would be as much my decision as his.' I'm inclined to say that it's clear who wears the trousers in her marriage, but keep a diplomatic silence. 'Unless you tell Mum what's going on, we can't help. Simple as that. I'll speak to Mum—' She cuts me off.

I leave the shop quickly, saying something about needing a couple of days for cheques to clear. The bus takes an age to arrive, then I don't have enough for the whole fare, so I get off at the Pier and almost run along the Promenade. There's a biting wind, but I'm soaked with perspiration by the time I turn into the hotel.

I hear Barbara's voice, excited, through the door, and catch her sitting at the table, speaking to her iPad. Blast, I must have left it out. She turns, flushes, and says, 'Goodbye, darling, your dad's here'.

She brings my carpet slippers and takes my coat. I tell her I've been to the estate agent, to see if there was any possibility of a better price on the house.

'Oh, Harry, two pieces of good news at once. Things are looking up. That was Andrea on *Face2Face* just now. She's coming over. Ben's going to look after the children and she's getting the first flight she can.'

'I thought Ben was in the city on business.'

The bridge of her nose creases slightly. 'He's coming back today. Well, it's tonight, there, of course.' She hangs up my coat, puts on the kettle, arranges cups. 'You were quite flushed when you came in but now you're very pale. It's being cooped up here. Anyway, tell me your news. How did you get on with the estate agent?'

I say something non-committal about needing to cash in an investment, and she bustles about, making toast and coffee, humming some tune I recognize from The Pirates of Penzance. The iPad pings and she prods at it, then speaks to the screen.

'Andrea, darling.'

I hear my daughter's tinny voice. 'Tomorrow evening, Mum, can't wait to see you.' And then she's gone.

'Why the sudden rush for Andrea to visit?' I ask.

'She didn't say. But she always was spontaneous. It'll be lovely. But,' she looks around our crowded and dingy room. 'Where will she sleep?'

'I'll book her a room, don't worry.'

'You will? Thank you, Harry. Now then – should we bring a few things from the storage unit to put around the place? Make it more homely? A few family photos, and that Maori rug they sent for Christmas?'

'Sure. Why don't we both go? We'll go after lunch.'

'You mean it? That would be lovely, Harry. I'd like to see my things again.'

As we walk through the foyer, I hail Sam or

Seth and say, 'A day or so at the most.'

Barbara tries to take my hand. 'Really, Harry, so fast?'

I put my fingers in my collar to loosen it. 'I made a few arrangements this morning, so, yes, I think we can safely say that by the time Andrea gets here, we'll have some news. In fact, if she's around for a few days, she could help us to move.' My wife looks as though she could walk to the moon and back. It makes me love her and hate her, in the same breath. 'Shall we walk up to the industrial estate? I know it's quite a distance, but the wind has dropped and the sun is out, and you're right, I'm not feeling very fit. I know some short cuts to keep us off the main road. It'll be good exercise.'

This is how I want to remember my wife: in her own armchair, surrounded by the story of us. A stack of photograph albums on the floor beside her: our wedding day; Andrea growing up, her graduation, her wedding to Ben, George's christening. Our visit to them five years ago, and theirs to us last year. The

Maori rug. On the table, a scatter of magazines and on her lap, a novel. At her feet, her basket is overflowing with knitting and embroidery projects, and her hand is reaching down as if she is about to decide which to work on next. Held tight in her other hand is a piece of wood which I think is the handle of one of my carpentry tools, but I can't open her fingers to make her let go. I look for the smile, but there is only that crease across the bridge of her nose, judging me, reminding me that I am a failure. I brush her hair and watch the little curls spring back. She looks cold, so I tuck the rug in around her. I wait for her to open her eyes and look at me. She doesn't. I sit, watching, waiting for the pressure to drain away. It doesn't. I put on my coat and check my pockets to be sure I have the swipe card which will let me out of the customer entrance. As I turn to leave, I see the hammer on the rug, and pick it up, wipe it, place it in the wooden box with the rest of my carpentry tools and tuck the box under my arm. I pull the door of the container closed behind me. The padlock snaps shut. As I walk away, along the silent steel corridor, I drop the key down a drain.

Second Honeymoon

Muttering under her breath, each angry phrase driving her forward, she marched through the lobby and out of the door. What an anniversary. Call this a second honeymoon?

After just a few steps, her forehead started throbbing and a wave of nausea pressed against the back of her teeth. Behind her, the door swished open and the cool breeze of air conditioning hit her legs.

The concierge called, 'Taxi, Madame?'

Swallowing the nausea, shaking her head, she kept walking across the hotel forecourt. Ahead, the tops of the Pyramids were just visible above the line of stationary traffic. The stench of diesel burned her nostrils. Perspiration trickled between her breasts and her sunglasses slipped down her nose.

A wizened man in a galabeya blocked her way. 'Carriage, lady?' Her eyes followed the reins, held in one hand, to an emaciated horse.

She stepped around him. 'No, thank you.'

'Pyramid? Sphinx? Special fix price.' He walked beside her, yanking the horse along behind him.

She stepped off the pavement, weaving between vehicles, losing his voice in the cacophony of revving engines, blaring horns and shouting.

It felt so different to the first time, their real honeymoon. Everything had changed. Or perhaps not. Maybe it was her memory that had changed the original, coloured it in with a rosy tint, like touching up an old photograph. Whatever made her think a second honeymoon could save this marriage? The belly dancing outfit was the final straw. It was over. Time to call time. At the thought of calling time, she pictured Kevin as she had left him, slumped and scowling, in the balcony bar.

The whole thing had been a mistake: the first honeymoon, the marriage, everything. She'd fallen for the dream, talked herself into the romance of marriage; relished being the first of her friends to find the perfect man. They all swooned over Kevin, and he chose her. Kevin, her David Essex lookalike with his curly black hair and cheeky grin. Mum and Dad were so proud when their flibbertigibbet daughter found herself a man with prospects. And the wedding truly was the best day of her life. Afterwards, she missed her friends, but marriage was a welcome escape from the tedium of the typing pool. For a while, she was happy to trade cooking, cleaning, even sex, for the fear of being left on the shelf.

The trickle of sweat reached her navel and ran around her knicker elastic, where it joined another rivulet descending from between her shoulder blades, so that one hot, sticky river encircled her stomach.

Hands flapped in front of her face, wrapping a scarf around her shoulders. 'Ten pounds only.' She shrugged it off. The hands wrapped it around her head. 'I make you look like queen.'

Fingers snapped in her face. 'One euro?' and she looked down on a small boy swinging cheap bracelets from his hands.

Pushing the scarf from her head, she kept moving forward, repeating, 'No, thank you, no,' to left and right. Shrill voices and stick-like arms waving gewgaws followed her into the sandy road that led to the Pyramids. A stone bit into the ball of her foot, and she stumbled. With one hand against the wall, she pulled off her sandal. The traders surrounded her, their voices becoming a babble that bounced around her brain and thumped behind her eyes. It took her back to the bazaar that morning. Kevin had haggled with the traders while a crowd gathered, pointing from him to her, laughing. Whether it was the price he was offering, or because they imagined her wearing that ridiculous belly dancing outfit, she had squirmed with embarrassment. Later, she'd studied the phrasebook. It was worth a try.

Raising her hand, palm outward, she said, 'Laa, shukran.'

The traders melted away. Perhaps she'd said something else, something rude, should call them back, reassure them. Only the small boy remained, gazing silently at her. She pulled some change from her pocket, passed it to him. He selected four sparkling bracelets which he pushed onto her arm. She slipped her foot back into her sandal and resumed her walk. Approaching the entrance gate, she saw it was padlocked. Of course, it was late.

Across the busy road, the blue parasols of the

hotel roof bar merged with the darkening sky. Kevin probably hadn't even noticed her absence. He'd be past the self-righteous, argumentative stage, well into the maudlin phase. In his alcoholic fug, whatever he was unhappy about would be her fault. Sooner or later – tonight, tomorrow, next week – she would apologise, not even knowing why. Until she did, there'd be slamming and sulking and cutting remarks under his breath. She knew the pattern. For the first few years of their marriage he'd kept it up for weeks. Until she learned. Making amends, keeping the peace, became easy, part of the job: putting the children to bed early, she'd be standing beside a bottle of Beaujolais and a T-bone steak as he came through the door. He'd look her up and down, detecting the shape of the slinky basque, his gift to her, beneath her tight jumper and jeans… and everything would return to normal. Until the next time.

Of course, she could have left, but for the children. Compared with the alternative – that half-life of low paid work and weekend visits from their father, that so many of her friends experienced after divorce – it seemed worth tolerating Kevin's faults. Now, the thought of time lost – twenty-five years! – made her catch her breath. A quarter century of anticipating, negotiating, bargaining. Fliss was right. Marriage was a form of prostitution. Fliss, the single parent friend she'd met at playgroup, who Kevin had banned from the house. She missed Fliss, with her tales of how she'd travelled the world, her baby in a sling, what she'd seen, who she'd met. Friendship with Fliss: something else she'd traded for what had seemed to be a better offer.

The Pyramids seemed to grow more enormous every second as the sun dropped behind, edging their profiles with a pink haze. She felt so small, with her trivial worries and preoccupations – choosing a new washer-tumbler, waiting for a call or a text from children busy with their own lives. It all suddenly seemed irrelevant, compared to the scale of this place, this moment. Surely there was more in life. It struck her that this could be her opportunity, to travel, to see the world. The kids don't need me. How different would this trip be, with Fliss? Perhaps I can find her...

The boy tugged at her dress. 'You like tea, Madame?' He pointed to a shop-front. It looked closed, but as they approached, she saw figures moving behind the grubby window. The boy's hand in hers, she stood at the door. A group of men drank coffee in the corner while at a table, women smoked pipes which she thought her daughter once told her were called bongs; but they could hardly be smoking marijuana in public, could they? She found herself sitting at a table. A man placed a glass of steaming water in front of her and pressed a handful of mint leaves into it. As she sipped, the aromas of mint, spice and incense filled her mind with, yes, it was joy. Peace and joy. That was the kind of thing Fliss would say. She giggled and looked up to find a woman watching, her eyes twinkling from her burqa.

The boy had gone. An older man sat at her table, smiling with beautiful, even teeth, reminding her of... Kevin, but the Kevin of her memories, with his dark curls, olive complexion and even white teeth. Sipping the mint tea, she thought, if only he hadn't spent the intervening years in a drunken, sulking stupor, becoming blotchy and overweight...

Leaning towards her husband's alter ego, she listened to his musical, broken English as he told her about his dreams.

*

Slumped across the table in the Sphinx bar, scowling at Judy's untouched cocktail, he waggled his fingers in the air and ordered another double whisky. Was it two, or three whiskies since she went to the toilet? Where had the silly bitch got to?

He took the glass from the waiter, swirled the drink, examined it. 'Call it Scotch? More like camel piss.' He knocked it back, then stood, swayed, steadied himself. The waiter held out the bill. He snatched it, scribbled on the bottom and dropped it on the table. He picked up Judy's glass and raised it to the dark sky. 'Up yours, darling'. He drained it in two long swallows, handed the glass to the waiter and weaved out of the empty bar.

Outside his room, unable to fit his key card into the slot, he rested his forehead against the door and knocked with both fists. A passing room service boy picked up the card from the floor and opened the door.

Inside, he leaned on the door to close it, taking in the cool darkness and the quiet whirr of the air conditioning. He belched, then chuckled at an image of

Judy: lying on the bed, waiting for him, wearing the belly dancing kit he'd bought at the Khan el Khalili bazaar this morning. She'd stared at him with a face like a slapped arse, but he knew she'd like it. He hiccupped. 'Little minx. You know how to get around me.' Arms outstretched, he felt his way along the short lobby. When the wall ended, he lost his balance and fell, sprawling onto the bed. Within seconds, he was snoring.

He woke with his tongue stuck to the roof of his mouth. Rasping his hand across his chin, he groaned, 'Pass me the water'. Receiving no response, he sat up slowly and looked around. Apart from the creases in the cover where he had lain, the bed was neatly made up. He crossed to the window and pulled back the drapes, shielding his eyes against the sudden, strong sunlight. Judy was not on the balcony. He stumbled to the bathroom. 'Coming in.' Unzipping his fly, he flicked out his penis, leaning his head against the wall. The dark yellow stream of urine hit the shallow porcelain toilet bowl, droplets bouncing over the side and onto his shoe. He pulled up his trousers, turned and saw that he was alone. He checked the bedroom and the balcony again. His stomach rumbled. He looked at the clock and saw it was nearly midday. Of course, she'd be having lunch.

He walked through the restaurant, his eyes skimming the tables, and into the foyer. The concierge approached, smiling, 'Can I help, sir?'

'My wife is not in our room.'

'You stay in this hotel, sir?'

'Yes, of course, you see me every day.'

'Room number?'

He held out his key card. The concierge raised a hand and caught the attention of a desk clerk, saying something in rapid Arabic.

The clerk's fingers flashed over the touch-screen. 'You check out, sir?'

'No, stay two more days.' He unconsciously aped the skeletonised English.

'No, sir, I mean guest in this room have check out.'

He ran his tongue around his teeth to unglue his lips and spoke louder. 'Have you seen my wife?'

The clerk frowned, looked at his screen and

repeated, louder, 'Guest in this room have check out. Sir.' He swivelled the monitor around and pointed: room number, final bill, marked as paid.

'Don't be ridiculous. I'm here aren't I? How can I have checked out?'

The desk clerk shrugged, clearly at the end of his repertoire. A group of people stood beside suitcases, watching him. A young girl stood open-mouthed and, following her gaze, he zipped up his fly and pulled his shoulders back. He turned to the concierge.

'Did you see my wife last night?'

'Sorry, sir. I think I do not know your wife.'

Fighting a desire to grab the man by the neck and shake him until he found some different words, he breathed deeply and said, very slowly, 'My wife is missing. We have not checked out.'

He grabbed his key card from the concierge and strode towards the spiral staircase leading to the bedroom corridor. The concierge followed.

Entering the room, he saw immediately that the surfaces were bare. 'Oops, wrong room.' About to turn away, he noticed something through the half-open wardrobe door and pulled it open. A monogrammed handkerchief, a long-ago Christmas gift from one of his children, lay on the floor. The empty hangers tinkled as he slammed the door shut. In the bathroom was only the hotel's toiletry pack. Standing in the middle of the room, looking around for any sign of Judy, he noticed the safe door was ajar and walked across. It was empty. Suddenly cold, shivering, he went out to the balcony to feel the warmth of the sun. The concierge picked up the telephone.

He sat on the balcony, drumming his fingers on the arm of the plastic chair. Maybe he should search the hotel? Everyone knew how dangerous these places could be. Especially since the revolution; it had made things worse, if anything. It had been a stupid decision to come here. Why was he sitting, doing nothing, more or less under guard by that damned concierge with his oily smile, who he'd spoken to every day and now flatly denied seeing him before. He slapped his hands on the arms of the chair, stood and turned, meeting a police officer in the doorway.

'About time, my wife has been kidnapped…'

The policeman stepped onto the balcony. 'Sir, you have passport? Identification?'

'No, I already explained to him over there, my wife and all my belongings are gone.' Really, he thought, these people.

'Passport, please, Sir.'

'Oh, for goodness sake.' He pushed against the police officer's arm and found himself grasped firmly by the elbow.

The officer spoke in almost perfect English. 'We telephone the airport. The lady and gentleman who were staying in this room must return to the UK urgently. They leave Egypt this morning. It is illegal to occupy a hotel room without correct registration. As you have no identification you must come with me.'

*

The doors slid open and she stepped into the Arrivals area, exhaling long and slow, feeling the fear seep away as oxygen flowed through her bloodstream, filling her with excited anticipation. She turned to her companion who smiled and, bowing slightly, took her hand and kissed it. About to let her hand drop, she paused, then tugged his white shirt cuff from his sleeve. Reaching into her bag with the other hand she pulled out a pen, and wrote a telephone number on his cuff. She pulled the two large suitcases towards the sign for the car parks, turning at the lift doors to give him a small wave.

Sand

I killed my little brother. When he was two, and I was six, I crept into his bedroom and suffocated him with a pillow while he slept.

'No you didn't, Nadine,' said my mother, 'It's a dream.'

'It's a dream about guilt,' my psychiatrist said, patting me on the knee. 'You mustn't blame yourself, my dear, it wasn't your fault.'

On Tuesdays, I go to the Community Clinic for my weekly meeting with parents who are thought to present a risk to their children. Publicly, it's called a 'parents' support group' so they have a cover story when they come into reception. But these mums and dads are under no illusions; they watch me scribbling notes and know my risk assessment will dictate their future. If they give the right response, the courts may grant them a family life; the wrong answers and they won't see their children again; something in between and they could get one afternoon a fortnight at a contact centre where, corralled by cuddly toys, they will try to engage their little strangers in a parody of play, under the watchful eye and busy pen of a social worker. While this process grinds slowly forward, the children who are being protected will metamorphose into sullen teenagers with unmet needs who will probably follow the pattern of their parents, having children of their own who will be in need of protection; and the circle will start again.

Jay-zee tells the group that she didn't burn her baby's feet with cigarettes. Gareth says, 'Bollocks' and Jay-zee's face turns blotchy with the shock that someone who should be on her side has let her down. I know she's lying, but the power of the group is that they can challenge one another more effectively than I ever could. Jay-zee jumps up, kicks back her chair and turns to Gareth, her hand pulled back into a fist, then catches sight of me. She knows she's blown it, and storms out, a middle finger waving in the air behind her.

In a practiced segue, Jay-zee is forgotten and all eyes turn to the next person seated clockwise in the circle. Jason went to prison for hitting his child. It was an accident – he meant to hit his girlfriend but she was holding the toddler at the time. So it was her fault the child was injured. This was the story he stuck to as he sat in isolation, trying to shut out the voices of other prisoners passing his cell door, whispering, 'Nonce… nonce…'. On film night, they let him join the others, and a prisoner offered Jason a drink. Another held him while he drank it. It's hard to listen to Jason's voice as it struggles through his bleached vocal chords, telling us about his guilt. I stop him after five minutes, and Gareth, seated next to him, slaps him on the shoulder in a gesture of solidarity and starts his own story. It's like a macabre version of a game of Consequences.

After clinic, on Tuesday nights, I dream new ways of killing my brother. I strangle him with my school tie until his eyes bulge and his pink tongue falls onto his rosy lips. I push him headlong into a puddle and hold his head under water until the bubbles stop rising and his chubby heels stop splashing. I know it isn't true. The real story was recorded by police and counsellors, recounted by my parents and, in the present generation, it's the family tragedy narrated by my own children. This is only a dream, I tell myself, night after night, as Carl's face shifts in the shadows of the dawn, creeping across my bedroom floor, shattering against my outstretched hand.

It's a summer Sunday at the seaside. The sun is pale and weak, but we insist on wearing our bathing suits. Mine is a navy blue ruched swimsuit, Carl has grey woollen trunks, knitted by Mummy, and black plimsolls. Carl and I play in the dunes. The stiff breeze dances the marram grass and draws sandy swirls around my feet. I hear Mummy calling, 'Nadine. Carl. Fooood'. Tugging on a handful of grass I pull myself up to the tip of the dune. Miles of golden beach and grey-green sea stretch before me. Bright balls bounce, children splash and scream and run in and out of the waves. I can see Daddy, kneeling, setting out our picnic where the sand turns from golden to dark brown, battered hard and smooth by the outgoing tide. Mummy is waving her arms above her head, and I wave back. A gust of wind blows stinging sand into my eyes and I squeal and rub with the heels of my hands, and I am falling, rolling down the dune. Then Mummy has hold of me, pulling first one eye open, then the other, blowing the gritty sand away. Now I'm sitting on the tartan rug. Daddy presses a sandwich into one hand, a beaker and straw into the other. Eggy cress squeezes onto my fingers from between the thin white slices. Tizer fizzes on my lips.

Mummy says, 'Where's Carl?' Her eyes, shaded by her hands, retrace my journey across the dunes. I shrug and point towards a group of children whose multi-coloured kites slice through the candy floss clouds, then point the other way, to the line of donkeys. 'When can I have my ride?' I ask, but she isn't listening. She's running away from me, her feet slipping and sliding on the soft-piled sand of the dune. Pulling off her sandals, she throws them away from her and climbs, head forward, elbows sticking out, looking like Jiminy Cricket. 'Carl-Carl,' she's shouting.

Daddy is on his feet. He wags a finger at me, says, 'Stay there,' and is off, running along the line of wrack at the edge of the sea. He pauses, peering at a group of children splashing in the surf, then turns to the mother who is unscrewing a thermos flask clenched between her knees. 'Have you seen a small boy?' he says. She stares up at him. He tuts and puffs and runs on.

There's a mighty crash from the waves. The clouds have fallen into the sea. I hear a low rumble. It might be the Jelafish coming to get me. It's getting louder. I scream and drop my beaker; there's an orange Tizer puddle on the rug. Daddy runs back to me. Heavy drops of water splash onto my head, my sandwich, the rug. It's pouring down. Daddy looks towards Mummy, now at the top of the dune, still calling, 'Carl-Carl'. He throws a towel over my head and runs in the other direction. I sit there for a long time, staring from beneath the towel at the low grey waves. Jelafish is sucking in the pebbles, chewing them noisily then spitting them out. I tuck my feet under my bottom so it can't grab my toes and pull me in. Water is running off my head onto my sandwich. The eggy mess drips from my fingers onto my knees. I start to shiver.

A policeman takes me by the hand. He drops it

and, taking out a handkerchief, wipes the sludgy remains of my sandwich from his fingers, then picks up my hand again. He is carrying Mummy's handbag under his arm. I can't see Mummy or Daddy. People are lined, still and quiet, along the tide line. Kites dangle from small hands. People fall back as I walk past. I watched Princess Anne in a procession like this on the television. Perhaps I should wave.

We still lived in the seaside town, but we never went to the beach again. We stayed at home in case Carl came back or someone called with news of him. I spent long hours in my brother's room, which changed and grew with the ageing of his ghost. My father continued to fill the shelves with books and games, ready for the day the infant, junior, or teenage Carl came home. Model planes that Carl had not yet known circled me as I lay on his bed and read: Kidnapped, Treasure Island, Swiss Family Robinson. I closed my eyes and fell asleep watching my little brother, still running along that endless golden beach, laughing over his shoulder. I killed my little brother, I said, I know I did. No, you didn't, Nadine, it's just a dream.

There was a process of attrition. During the day, my parents went through the motions of keeping home and work together, but, waking during the night – from The Dream – I would find my mother in the kitchen. Her forehead resting on the kitchen table, hands grasping, she called out from her drugged sleep to the crying child that only she could hear. Eventually, the tranquillizers relieved her of any remaining capacity to interact with the world around her, while Father, greying and stooped, merged with the shadows as he continued to search the streets night after night. Conjoined in guilt, mining their memories for faults, their haunted faces collapsed into the years. Meantime, on the table, on the mantelpiece, on the walls, Carl's blond, blue-eyed innocence gazed from a perfectly framed past. My parents were hollowed out by a grief that lived and breathed beside us. I was taken aback one day, when I found the four of us, laughing together in a family snapshot. I placed it in the memory box that I would share with Carl one day.

This Tuesday, Gareth tells us about his ghosts. Aged fourteen, he listened as his father killed his mother. Heard him come to the house, late, drunk, hammering his fists on the door until, to stop the neighbours from complaining, she let him in. 'I'm a coward,' Gareth says. 'I should've protected her.' He hid beneath his bed, retching to the rhythmic crunch as the kitchen chair broke her bones. His father is serving life. Gareth pledged to find him and kill him. But his threats are taken to mean his baby is in danger. I believe Gareth. My job is to help him, and others for whom there is hope, to tell their stories and be believed. This group is a place where Gareth can reinvent himself. Much as I did. Long years of counselling cured me of the belief that I had harmed my brother, helped me to reinvent myself, and enthused me to help others do the same. This is how my profession found me. I work with guilt. I help the guilty to live with it, the innocent to survive it and the remorseless to find it.

I don't know when my parents lost hope, but one day, they did stop watching and waiting. They appeared to outsiders to be conscientious and caring, encouraging me in my school and netball triumphs, always where they needed to be, telling the world they did not blame me. My graduation photos show them proudly smiling. Perhaps they were celebrating having served out their sentence of duty to me. The very next day, I found them dead together, empty blister packs of tranquillizers stacked neatly on the bedside table.

Clearing the house, I found the story of Carl in a box of photos, cuttings and correspondence. 'Mystery of Missing Toddler': the search went on for months. In those days, dogma had it that women were most likely to abduct small children, and the press targeted women who were childless or bereaved, presumed thwarted and unfulfilled and therefore dangerous. Neighbours were invited to report women seen in the company of unidentified children; strangers felt able to challenge middle aged women walking with children in the street; child-minders' homes were raided. A spirit medium wrote to my parents describing Carl as doted on and doting, in a new life far away. Our holidays were spent following these leads, standing outside strangers' houses in far away cities and towns. Me, with Mummy or Daddy, never both, for someone had to stay at home, just in case.

Professionally, I discovered what my parents could not have known. That on any summer Sunday, in any seaside town, paedophiles enjoy the fleeting and superficial delights of mixing, undetected, with the objects of their fantasies; there are children everywhere. Camouflaged as ordinary folk, avuncular and self-effacing, these men insinuate themselves into groups of holidaymakers, carefully selecting and grooming parents and grandparents as they move ever closer to their prey. I have often wondered who was watching, waiting beside the dunes that day, ready to pluck Carl from my family tree? Did my little brother suffer horrors at their hands or live his life as someone's plaything? Did he wait in hope that I would come and rescue him, while his memories of home faded and were eventually forgotten?

Today, my neighbour tells me that something is happening at the beach; she says police are everywhere. From the car park, I see blue and white tape fluttering on the dunes. As I approach, a police officer says, politely, 'You can't come any further madam'. Two small boys, identically freckled beneath ginger crew-cuts, stand shivering in a family group nearby, plastic spades dangling from their fingers. Resting on a tussock of marram grass is a piece of black rubber, a scrap of canvas attached. Beside it, a small pile of bleached sticks and a tiny, burnished skull. The police officer says, 'Are you all right, madam?'

It's a summer Sunday at the seaside. The sun is pale and weak, but we insist on wearing our bathing suits. Mine is a navy blue ruched swimsuit, Carl has grey woollen trunks, knitted by Mummy, and black plimsolls. A stiff breeze dances the marram grass and draws sandy swirls around my feet. Carl's white-blond head sticks out of the sand and he says, 'Bury me, Neddie,' as I pat it down tight around his chin. 'More, more,' he yells, so I push sand up to his ears and tuck it around his head so that just his face is peeping out. He giggles, delighted. I hear Mummy calling, 'Nadine. Carl. Fooood'. Tugging on a handful of grass I pull myself up to the tip of the dune. Miles of golden beach and grey-green sea stretch before me. Bright balls bounce, children splash and scream and run in and out of the waves. I can see Daddy, setting out our picnic. Mummy is waving her arms above her head, and I wave back. I think I hear Carl calling, 'Neddie,' but when I turn around, I can't see where his voice is coming from. A gust of wind blows stinging sand into my eyes. I cannot see, I am falling, rolling down the dune.

The Last Post

Monday 5th December

I'm looking forward to getting back to work today after my day off, although I feel a little guilty, leaving Winston all alone. There he sits, beside his litter tray, gazing sadly at me as I leave. I can't trust Daddy to give him any attention. Winston has never forgotten being abandoned the time Daddy was found wandering on the railway line. With all the kerfuffle involving police and hospitals and social workers, he was all alone in the empty house for nearly a week.

Today is one of those sunny but brisk autumnal days, so I'm glad of my new regulation fleece jacket – it's very smart and warm – and I have made sure to take my echinacea and vitamin supplements to fend off winter coughs and colds. Fortunately, I live barely five minutes' walk from the Sorting Office, so within half an hour I've picked up my post bag and am back home. As I reach the gate, Mrs Pettifer in Flat 6 taps on her window and beckons me inside. She wants me to put her bin out for collection tomorrow. Of course I will, she doesn't need to ask, but it is nice not to be taken for granted. She is a bit of a chatterbox though, asking me about Winston, and how Daddy is, and so it's later than usual before I get into my own flat, and unpack my bag.

I count out the envelopes into piles, C4, C5, and so on, 208 altogether. There are a few parcels that are small enough to go letter-post. And some plain white envelopes which I think are early Christmas cards. Oh, and two of those padded jobs, which now count as packets. When it all changed to price-by-size instead of just by weight it was a boon to my job, I can tell you. It's difficult to push those C4 envelopes through the letter box without bending the corners. Those letter boxes with the little draught excluder brushes make it particularly difficult. Nowadays, it's cheaper to use C5 envelopes and fold the contents, making it bulkier and easier to handle. It's fair, to price for size as well as weight, even though it has doubled the time it takes me to check the mail. I asked Mr Dickson, my supervisor, if I could have one of those red, plastic sizing templates such as they use in the office. He gave me an odd look, but he did give me one. No doubt he's pleased to know someone in his team takes the job seriously.

So it is an exceptionally heavy mail this morning, and by the time I've checked all the envelopes against my sizing template and the list of postage rates, and what with Mrs Pettifer wanting to talk, I'm quite behind. It's nearly eight o'clock before I'm able to start delivering the post and I have to rush to fit it all in and get back in time to clock off and get home to feed Winston and Daddy. Not that he's hungry and I have to throw it in the bin again. It being Monday, I spend the rest of the day doing the washing, and changing Daddy's bedding. I am very proud of my hospital corners, done just the way Mummy taught me.

Tuesday, 6th December

There are 273 envelopes, and no C4s at all. I wonder whether that size will become as rare as foolscap. I mean, you don't see much foolscap around these days, do you? There are three official envelopes for number 18, with typed address labels and no sender's details. One of them is a window envelope and I tap it on my palm to try to move the letter up or down, but it is a tight fit and I'm unable to see much. Of course, there's a brown envelope for one of the Burtons. I recognize by the franking that it's from the benefits office.

I have a parcel of my own, today. It isn't addressed to my real name of course. I don't like my colleagues at the Sorting Office to know my business. It's a delivery of glucosamine from Vitco. I remember from last winter how the cold weather plays havoc with Daddy's joints. I used to swear by cod liver oil. Then, I found an article about glucosamine in the Sunday paper and ordered some. I go in to Daddy and show him, but he just stares at me. Well, if that's how you feel, I think to myself, I'll leave you to your thoughts. He seems to spend a lot of time thinking, these days, and I hope he's reflecting on his ill-spent years. Even so, I keep thirty tablets back in case he changes his mind, and divide the remainder into eight equal portions which I drop into eight padded envelopes. Across the top I write: Free Sample. I put these envelopes in the front of my post bag so not to mix them up with the main mail. If I see any poor old soul on my route who seems to be suffering with their joints, I shall post them through their letter box.

Mrs Bishop gives me a cheery wave from the window as I pass her house. She's looking much better. I thought she was a little peaky last week, so I dropped a packet of Mega Mineral Complex through her letter box. I packaged it well because she has a little terrier that tears the post to pieces before it has even landed on the mat. Mrs Bishop is an old friend of my mother so I like to do what I can.

On my way home, I call into Thorpe's Hardware. I've had my eye on an electronic scale. It can be my Christmas present to myself. Back in our street, I find the dustbins all awry on the pavement. I worry about how the old folk get along the pavement on a Tuesday, with bins all over the show and litter scattered around. The refuse collection hasn't been of the same standard since the Council contracted it out to companies who only want to make a profit. It's the same in the Post Office since privatization. After I've tidied up and made it all spick and span again, Mrs Pettifer knocks on her window and raises a thumb, so obviously she thinks so too. I tell Daddy that I intend to write to the Council and complain, but as usual, he isn't interested. This afternoon, as it's Tuesday, I dust and polish all my surfaces, and can't help noticing how much more onerous this is, since Winston moved in.

Wednesday 7th December

There are a lot of packages today. People will be getting their Christmas shopping organized. This internet shopping business has changed the face of the postal service. It was a worry, when that web thing first started up; we all thought the post office would go out of business. But on the contrary, we've had something of a comeback, because everything people buy on the internet has to be delivered. These parcels come in all sizes and shapes, and some of them arrive in a terrible state. And there's no allowance made for us carrying these bulky parcels around. Mr Dickson offered me a bicycle but I told him, I suffer from vertigo. Some of the older posties have been issued with little trolleys.

Our shop steward says these innovations are just to make us do more for the same wages. But when Mr Dickson gave us a pep talk last week he said that now we've been privatized we have targets to think of if we're not to lose our share of the market. He said there's plenty of competition, with all those courier services out there; the customer has the choice and they won't choose us if we're inefficient. The shop steward had something to say about that point of view, but as Mr Dickson said, the union won't give me a job if the Post Office goes out of business, will it? On balance I think Mr Dickson's right. We have to do our best and I shall do my bit. I'll ask him how I can apply for a trolley of my own.

My new electronic scales work very well. Today I find two underpaid letters that haven't been noticed at the Sorting Office. They can be very slipshod in that department. I don't collect the money from the customers. I just write it on the envelope so they know it's underpaid. Then they can tell the sender to get it right next time.

With all this extra workload, I forgot to give Daddy his breakfast, so I call at the Spar on my way home and buy him a beef and ale pie, which I know to be one of his favourites. Who should I bump into but the daughter of that woman who lived on his corridor in the care home. She asks after Daddy and I tell her he's very well. I can't remember her name or her mother's name, but I do remember the day I visited and found him entertaining her in his room. I tried to tell him about my research into herbal medication that might benefit his diabetes, but he was not at all attentive to me, having eyes only for his new lady friend. She batted her eyelashes at him as though she was sixty years younger. I could see he was lining up yet another stepmother for me. That's when I decided he should come home to live with me. We haven't seen eye to eye over the years, especially not after he left Mummy and me for that girl who was barely older than me. But blood's thicker than water, and being back home, with me and mother, might make him realize how he's deprived himself of a family life by playing fast and loose and spending all his money on drink and dogs. And of course, this way, I can make sure he doesn't do anything silly again.

I get home to find Winston standing on the

draining board looking out of the window, making those little squeaks that usually mean he's seen a bird that he'd quite like to play with. Sure enough there is a robin sitting on the washing line. I don't like Winston to get too excited before his meal, so I tap on the window and shoo the bird away. Then I notice one of those Burton scamps at their window, which overlooks my kitchen. He is pointing at me and laughing. There are a few things I could say about that family, with their final notices for electricity and whatnot. You can tell when the children in that family reach eighteen because they start getting brown envelopes of their own. I draw the blind and switch on the radio, quietly, so not to disturb Daddy. There is no sound from his room so he must be asleep. I shall eat the steak and ale pie myself and then, it being a Wednesday, need to get on with the hoovering.

Thursday 8th December.

There's a letter addressed to Daddy from his doctor, inviting him in for his annual health check and reminding him that he missed it last year. I put the letter through the shredder. There are also 47 Christmas cards in my bag, so it's time to get my special notebook out. I keep a record of who's getting what so I can send cards to those who don't get any. I like to make sure everyone on my round gets at least one card.

Later, when I've finished my delivery, I call into the newsagent to buy a bumper pack of cards. The lady at the till says, got a big family have you, duck? She says this every year. The week before Christmas, I'll be up all night writing them out and walking all over town to post them in different locations. When the envelopes land in my bag for delivery, I recognize my own handwriting, and get a certain satisfaction from noting how long it has taken the Sorting Office to process them. They don't know the card is from me, of course. I sign it with a squiggle and leave it to their imagination. Mostly it's old folk and they probably think it's a friend from past times who they've forgotten. I miss off the foreign names in case they're not Christians. I wouldn't want to offend anyone.

Mr Burton is getting into his car as I deliver his mail. He calls out, here comes the Snail Mail, and laughs. The cheek of it. I tell him, our District met all our delivery time targets last year. I won't repeat what he said to me. I can see it's a new car and wonder how he can afford that as I happen to know he's unemployed.

Mrs Pettifer is looking out for me. She taps on her window and waves in a very agitated manner. When I go in, she says we have a Peeping Tom. Seemingly a car has been parked across the street all morning, with two men watching our block. She says one went around the back and peered over the fence, and then the other went off and got bacon baps which they ate in their car. On the way out, I look across the road and sure enough there is a tomato ketchup sachet blowing in the gutter, so I pick it up.

While I'm doing the ironing, and putting the clothes away, I mention this to Daddy but he doesn't have anything to say on the matter. However, much later, when I'm pulling out the sofa bed, which I have to sleep on as Mummy and Daddy are using the bedroom, it occurs to me they might not be watching our block. It could be a good position for a discreet surveillance of those Burtons in the next street. Now that makes more sense.

Friday 9th December.

I am still unpacking the post onto the kitchen table ready for weighing and sorting, when the doorbell rings, accompanied by very loud knocking. My first thought is to get to the door quickly as I don't want Daddy woken too early. In my rush, I tread on Winston's tail. He shrieks and jumps onto the table, scattering packets and envelopes everywhere. I look along the hallway to the front door and then back at the mess and I don't know what to do first. Winston's hair on his spine is standing on end. Suddenly the door bursts open and three police officers run down the hallway. One pushes me against the wall. Another reaches for the electronic scales – he gets a nasty scratch from Winston's paw for his trouble. The other opens all the drawers and cupboards and empties the contents onto the floor. It is mayhem. He finds the packet of MCP powder which I'm planning to give to my father for Christmas. It is recommended for prostate problems. I try to tell him this but he laughs and nods to the officer holding me, who puts my hands behind my back and then I have handcuffs on, just like on the television, and he pushes me into a chair.

He tells me to keep quiet but then starts firing questions, so surely he expects me to answer him, but the questions are coming so fast that I barely open my mouth before he's on to the next.

We all know, one says, that only drug dealers use that kind of electronic scales. And those zip-lock bags. Well, I find my voice then and I tell him, there's nothing like that going on in this street, it's one of the best postcodes in the City. I start to tell him it's the Burtons who let the neighbourhood down, but I think he must already know that because he interrupts me. He waves some pills in front of my face and asks me what he'll find when they are tested at the laboratory. I start to tell him – vitamin supplements – but he interrupts me again. He says they're going to keep my little book with all the names and addresses and pay those people a visit. So I can't send Christmas cards this year. They are also going to take my scales away.

This goes on for some time, and eventually I realise they think I've been dealing drugs, and using my post bag to move them around. They've been watching my place, and even followed me for several days. They call the Sorting Office and Mr Dickson comes and says, yes, I am an employee. He stands in the kitchen, looking around at the mess of letters and parcels still lying on the table and the floor. He picks them all up and puts them into my postbag. He says someone else will deliver them. He says I can keep the sizing template.

There's a kerfuffle in the hallway and the police officer pulls me to my feet and pushes me along to the front door, and outside, where there is a crowd of people. The Burtons are watching, and Mrs Pettifer is sitting at her window. The officer presses me into the back seat of a police car and through the window I watch a little procession coming out of the house. Mr Dickson walks past, with my postbag. He is followed by a policeman holding Winston in a kind of headlock. Then comes the social worker, the one who didn't want Daddy to leave the care home. She has mother's silver urn in her hands, and is followed by two paramedics carrying a stretcher between them. I can't see Daddy; his face is covered with a blanket.

Thank you for reading this short story collection. Your feedback is appreciated – please leave a review; even if it's just a few words, it means a lot to the author.

About the author:

Kate Mitchell's first novel, *The House Fell on Her Head*, was published on Amazon in 2016 and became a #1 bestseller in the Historical Mystery genre. Her short stories have been published in magazines, anthologies and online. She is currently working on a second novel, *Flashback*. Kate's work is often categorised as literary noir, possibly drawing on many years' experience working in the criminal justice system and in social care. The author now lives in the Lincolnshire Wolds where she writes and keeps bees.

Follow Kate Mitchell on Twitter: @k8swaby

Printed in Great Britain
by Amazon

67949667R00076